The gunner stared at the Executioner with stark terror

Bolan placed the burning hot barrel of the Desert Eagle against his forehead, and the man recoiled in fear.

"I want to know what your shipment consisted of, where it is and when it is scheduled to be delivered to the Holy Voice."

"Malkani will kill me if I talk. If the Holy Voice doesn't get me first."

"Gadish didn't want to tell me, either," Bolan growled.

The man glanced down at the corpse, then made a startled sound as the door burst open and Salah Abi rushed inside, his Smith & Wesson pistol sweeping the room.

"You are quite a mess maker, my friend," he said.

"It's about to get messier, Abi."

"No! I'll tell you anything," the dealer cried. "Just don't shoot!"

"No. You'll tell me *everything*," Bolan said in a low voice. "Or I *will* shoot."

MACK BOLAN ®

The Executioner

#152 Combat Stretch
#153 Firebase Florida
#154 Night Hit
#155 Hawaiian Heat
#156 Phantom Force
#157 Cayman Strike
#158 Firing Line
#159 Steel and Flame
#160 Storm Warning
#161 Eye of the Storm
#162 Colors of Hell
#163 Warrior's Edge
#164 Death Trail
#165 Fire Sweep
#166 Assassin's Creed
#167 Double Action
#168 Blood Price
#169 White Heat
#170 Baja Blitz
#171 Deadly Force
#172 Fast Strike
#173 Capitol Hit
#174 Battle Plan
#175 Battle Ground
#176 Ransom Run
#177 Evil Code
#178 Black Hand
#179 War Hammer
#180 Force Down
#181 Shifting Target
#182 Lethal Agent
#183 Clean Sweep
#184 Death Warrant
#185 Sudden Fury
#186 Fire Burst
#187 Cleansing Flame

#188 War Paint
#189 Wellfire
#190 Killing Range
#191 Extreme Force
#192 Maximum Impact
#193 Hostile Action
#194 Deadly Contest
#195 Select Fire
#196 Triburst
#197 Armed Force
#198 Shoot Down
#199 Rogue Agent
#200 Crisis Point
#201 Prime Target
#202 Combat Zone
#203 Hard Contact
#204 Rescue Run
#205 Hell Road
#206 Hunting Cry
#207 Freedom Strike
#208 Death Whisper
#209 Asian Crucible
#210 Fire Lash
#211 Steel Claws
#212 Ride the Beast
#213 Blood Harvest
#214 Fission Fury
#215 Fire Hammer
#216 Death Force
#217 Fight or Die
#218 End Game
#219 Terror Intent

DON PENDLETON'S
THE EXECUTIONER®
TERROR INTENT

A GOLD EAGLE BOOK FROM
WORLDWIDE®

TORONTO • NEW YORK • LONDON
AMSTERDAM • PARIS • SYDNEY • HAMBURG
STOCKHOLM • ATHENS • TOKYO • MILAN
MADRID • WARSAW • BUDAPEST • AUCKLAND

First edition March 1997
ISBN 0-373-64219-9

Special thanks and acknowledgment to
Tim Somheil for his contribution to this work.

TERROR INTENT

Printed in U.S.A.

Any coward can fight a battle when he's sure of winning....
—George Eliot
1819-1880

It takes a coward to kill defenseless innocents, and a warped mind to do it in God's name. The twisting path will eventually lead the terrorists to my door, to fight a battle they won't survive.

—Mack Bolan

THE
MACK BOLAN®
LEGEND

Nothing less than a war could have fashioned the destiny of the man called Mack Bolan. Bolan earned the Executioner title in the jungle hell of Vietnam.

But this soldier also wore another name—Sergeant Mercy. He was so tagged because of the compassion he showed to wounded comrades-in-arms and Vietnamese civilians.

Mack Bolan's second tour of duty ended prematurely when he was given emergency leave to return home and bury his family, victims of the Mob. Then he declared a one-man war against the Mafia.

He confronted the Families head-on from coast to coast, and soon a hope of victory began to appear. But Bolan had broken society's every rule. That same society started gunning for this elusive warrior—to no avail.

So Bolan was offered amnesty to work within the system against terrorism. This time, as an employee of Uncle Sam, Bolan became Colonel John Phoenix. With a command center at Stony Man Farm in Virginia, he and his new allies—Able Team and Phoenix Force—waged relentless war on a new adversary: the KGB.

But when his one true love, April Rose, died at the hands of the Soviet terror machine, Bolan severed all ties with Establishment authority.

Now, after a lengthy lone-wolf struggle and much soul-searching, the Executioner has agreed to enter an "arm's-length" alliance with his government once more, reserving the right to pursue personal missions in his Everlasting War.

PROLOGUE

Abu Simbel, Egypt

The street merchants shouted when the battered brown van rolled into their midst without slowing. The engine whined as the driver downshifted, and a bent old woman tottered angrily out of its path. She cursed the driver as the vehicle missed her by inches and was about to pound on the window when her eyes met the angry stare of the man in the passenger seat. She recognized the silhouette of a gun barrel. Grabbing her pack of tourist trinkets, she scurried quickly into the nearest alley.

Behind the wheel, Eid Farid didn't see the merchants scattering away before the van. His eyes were searching beyond the crowds, into the dusty, broad stretches of open ground that served as a parking area beyond the tourist market. Between the retail stalls and the restaurants, he spotted a row of buses.

THEO BIRKE WIPED his brow with his handkerchief and sprawled back in his chair in the open-air restaurant. The sun beat on him mercilessly. His shirt was soaked with sweat under his arms and was sticky against his back. He regarded the plate of half-eaten *fuul*. He'd ordered it meatless but still couldn't bring himself to trust it, having become violently ill on Egyptian food upon arrival. This morning, feeling strong again, he had thought he was recovered. Now he wasn't so sure.

How had Andrew Birkenfeld endured this place, under much more primitive conditions, for three full years? Birkenfeld had been Theo Birke's great-great-grandfather, a German scholar who'd lived in and traveled through Egypt at the turn of the century, at a time when a mania about ancient Egyptian artifacts was sweeping Europe and some of the greatest archaeological expeditions were under way. Birke was traveling in his great-great-grandfather's footsteps almost ninety years later, and in a much-abbreviated time frame. He'd flown into Cairo a week earlier and taken a shuttle flight down to Luxor to meet up with a guided tour. That was where his food sensitivities had acted up, and instead of joining the tour group, he'd taken to his hotel bed. In the end he'd missed tours of both the Luxor and the Karnak temples. He had been determined to see the Valley of the Kings if it killed him. His ancestor Andrew Birkenfeld had actually worked as a digger and foreman in the valley for eighteen months.

Birke did go to the valley, though his memory of the place was mostly of colorless, dry dirt, which he had stooped over all day as his stomach continued cramping.

The tour group he had joined had driven to Aswân and today their bus had made the nearly three-hour drive to Abu Simbel. Thank God the bus had air-conditioning. But his trip to Egypt finally became memorable in a positive light for Birke at the moment he stood looking up at the magnificent, twenty-yard-tall rock figures of Ramses II.

He'd felt a little healthier and emotionally restored, and had decided to chance some Egyptian food for lunch. The grain dish was likely fine; he was probably imagining the hint of rot he tasted in it.

Pete and Joy Taylor, across the table, were just finishing up their Lake Nasser catfish as if enjoying a feast fit for a pharaoh. Just looking at the oily fish remains sitting in the hot sun made Birke queasy again.

Pete noticed and chuckled. "You'll be at full speed again soon. Ramses's Revenge lasts just a few days."

Theo tried to smile. "I need to get back in the bus and cool down."

"I think we'll be coming with you." Joy nodded to Sadiq Nasr, the tour guide, who was searching for his group.

"You've been having a good lunch?" Nasr asked as he approached, cheery as ever. "Fine. You too, Mr. Birke? Feeling better, I can tell. Now we must be getting back to the bus, though, to stay on schedule."

Birke wasn't feeling better. In fact, he was feeling worse with every passing second. When he stood, the desert heat engulfed him and he wanted to run not walk to the air-conditioned tour bus, but he waited patiently for Pete and Joy. The three of them strolled through the crowds of tourists and merchants, Joy pausing interminably to peruse a display of locally made ceramics. Birke was now having trouble breathing and went on without them.

But when he pushed at the bus door, it was locked. The driver, also out having his lunch, hadn't yet returned. The engine had been left running, and the cooled air from the air-conditioned unit was leaking between the seams in the door, teasing Birke. He leaned against the vehicle, feeling as if he might pass out.

EID FARID DROVE THE VAN slowly along the edge of the parking area, scoping out the buses and vans, in search of the ideal target. It had to be large and heavily populated. It had to be accessible from all sides. He patted the knee of the quiet, contemplative man next to him.

"Seyyed, you do a great thing for us," he reminded the man.

Seyyed looked at him with faraway, bewildered eyes, his lips moving. He had been praying to himself for four hours now. Farid hoped the strength of Seyyed's conviction wasn't waning.

The ideally situated bus was at the end and separated from the others by at least ten yards. But there was no one inside it. Just one pathetic tourist slumped against it as if he was exhausted from his day of pleasant strolls through the ancient scenery. Farid turned at the end of the lot, eyes peeled for police. He'd circle again, hoping one of the heavily boarded buses near the front of the lot had opened up. If not, he would be forced to take the van from the parking area for a while or risk rousing someone's suspicions.

WHEN BIRKE LOOKED UP, the driver was returning, wiping crumbs from his beard and regarding him with distinct worry. He grasped Theo's shoulder and spoke in sympathetic Arabic.

"I'm fine. I'll be okay, really. I just need to get inside."

The driver unlocked the door, and Birke jumped up the steps. He rushed to the back of the bus, where the air would remain the coolest as others boarded.

Pete and Joy climbed aboard, followed by Nasr and a contingent of the twenty or so tourists that made up the rest of the group. Everyone was either American or British and every voice on the bus spoke English.

Nasr was frowning as he counted heads. Two people were missing, and he was trying to determine who they were.

"Sandra and her husband," suggested one of the travelers, a recent retiree, like Pete and Joy.

The guide nodded vigorously and stepped off the bus, peering into the crowds for Sandra and her husband.

FARID BOUNCED HIS HAND on the steering wheel in frustration. There were no likely targets, and Seyyed was getting noticeably agitated. He might be on the verge of changing his mind. Farid was about to steer into a side street when he noticed that the bus on the end, the one that had moments earlier been empty, was now full. He let the van roll to a stop. Yes, there were twenty or more tourists on board, all obviously European or American. And the bus that had been nearest to it was now pulling away, making the target bus even more of a perfect island in the open.

"This is it!"

There were hisses of approval from the back of the van.

Farid took Seyyed's shoulder in a firm grip. "Now is your moment, my friend!"

Seyyed's eyes were full of fear.

"Go, do God's work, and join Him in heaven. Death for the glory of God is our greatest ambition."

Seyyed looked at the floor and didn't react. Farid jumped out of the van and walked around to the passenger door. He ushered the man to his feet and urged him in the direction of the bus.

As he jumped behind the wheel again, the side door of the van opened and three of his men stepped out, hiding their arms underneath traditional long robes. Farid pulled the van around in a wide quarter-circle, to the front of the target bus and at a distance of at least ten yards.

Seyyed was moving hesitantly, and Farid placed his Ingram submachine gun on his lap for easy access. Seyyed had to have realized that his fate was sealed. There was no point in turning back. At the first hint of dissension, he would be shot.

Seyyed almost came to a halt several paces from the bus, then a change visibly overcame him. His steps suddenly became sure and quick, and his chin raised. When he looked up, Farid swore he could see the glint of determination in his eyes.

Seyyed entered the bus.

BIRKE WATCHED Nasr disappear into the crowds and spotted a man in long, traditional robes strolling through the crowds with a distracted look. He wondered how the man could tolerate the heat wrapped in what were essentially layers of cotton blankets.

Then there was a woman running through the crowds, wearing such an expression of worry that Birke knew something was terribly wrong. She also wore a robe, her head wrapped in scarves, obviously looking for someone. She stood on her toes to see over people, and called out. She seemed to locate what she was looking for and was running to an old brown van. The woman launched herself at a tight knot of men beside the van, hitting them with her open hand and shouting, though inside the bus, under the rush of cool air, Birke couldn't hear a sound.

He felt compelled to help the woman, but any effort on his part would have been worse than useless since he didn't speak her language. Surely someone would come to her aid, whatever the emergency.

He leaned his head back and sighed. His clothes were drying and he was more comfortable with every passing second. He felt alive again.

That was when the man in the robe pushed open the door, stepped onto the bus and cold-bloodedly shot the driver in the chest with a handgun. The screaming started.

FARID SPOTTED Ara as he heard the muffled gunshot from within the bus.

"Stop it! Stop it!" the woman screamed, trying to snatch an Ingram from one of his men as he stepped out of the van. He was startled by her appearance but managed to hold on to the weapon.

"Eid, stop this right now!" she shouted as he jumped out.

Farid waved off his other men with a flick of his hand and grabbed her by the wrist. "How dare you seek to stop God's work!"

"This is not God's work! This is evil! Those are innocent people, and you're making yourself a murderer!"

"If I kill, it is with purpose—to send our message! To usher God into this land! You don't have the right to question such holy work!" His men were deploying around the perimeter of the strike zone. He wouldn't be robbed of the opportunity to witness his enterprise. "Get in the van and shut the door," he ordered.

"Stop this act before it happens! Save these people!" Ara clung to his robe.

"I cannot and I will not."

She grabbed his Ingram so quickly it took him off guard, and she stepped away from him, nesting the wire stock against her shoulder and gripping the submachine gun like someone who knew what to do with one. Farid knew Ara had been raised around guns, and though her father had probably never taught her how to fire one, she had seen enough to know what she was doing. She waved the muzzle end in his direction.

"I'll kill you unless you stop this operation right now," she said with a quavering voice.

Farid hid his anger. "Ara..." he said in a hopeless tone, raising his hand as if in a gesture of sorrow and stepping in her direction. His hand closed instantly on the barrel of the submachine gun, and he lifted it from her hands before she knew she'd lost control of it. Then the metal stock slammed into her skull. The layers of scarves couldn't protect her, and she crumpled to the ground, unconscious.

Farid lifted her from the pavement and hoisted her to the open side door of the van like a sack of barley, then ran to the front of the van.

"What's happening?"

"Nothing!" said the nearest man, but in that instant Farid heard another two rounds of gunfire from inside the bus.

"What was that?" Farid demanded. "What's he doing?"

None of his men had an answer. Farid evaluated the situation quickly. The shots had gone unheard by the masses of tourists and merchants. The ambient din of the place had masked the muffled sound.

Again came the retort of gunfire.

"He should have detonated by now!" one of the men exclaimed.

"I know!" Farid said. "Something's gone wrong!"

BIRKE FELT COLD HORROR filling him like ice water pouring into a glass. The Egyptian had turned the gun on the group of tourists. He said nothing, simply pointed at them, his face a mask of...sorrow? Then the driver, struggling to stay alive, had lurched to his feet and tried to tackle the gunman. There were more screams, and the two of them went to their knees in the aisle. There were shouts in Arabic and more gunfire. Then the gunman stood, pushing away the driver's body and shooting him again.

It was while the gunman was turning that Pete jumped out of his seat. His college boxing days were decades behind him, but he still knew how to throw a punch. His fist collided with the gunman's jaw and the man flew backward, his fall cushioned by the corpse of the driver. But his grip on the gun remained tight. Joy screamed when he leveled it at her husband.

NASR WAS LAUGHING at something Sandra's husband said at the moment the Egyptian in traditional robes put a hand on his chest to stop him from walking any farther. The Egyptian shook his head as if the gesture were sufficient explanation.

"What's happening?" Nasr asked in Arabic.

The man said nothing, but his eyes were burning.

"What's going on?" Sandra asked.

There was a muffled sound that Sadiq recognized as gunfire and when he looked at the bus he saw two bodies slumping to the ground.

"No!" Nasr cried in English, and burst past the man who had stopped him.

"Halt!" The Egyptian's hand went into his robes and emerged with a Browning Hi-Power, which he leveled at Nasr's back. "Halt or I'll shoot!"

The pistol blasted four times when Nasr didn't comply with the order, and instantly the crowd was an hysterical mass, fleeing in all directions.

The tour guide tumbled to the ground, but was up again in an instant, ripping open the doors to the bus.

Inside, the gunman turned the handgun away to face the new arrival. With two rounds fired at such close range, there was no hope for the victim.

FARID CURSED LOUDLY when he heard the gunfire and saw the panic that ensued. "Fools! What are they doing over there?"

"Maybe Seyyed changed his mind and tried to get off the bus," one of his men suggested.

Farid cursed again and started to run, blasting at the ground with his pistol to clear a path through the panicked crowd now streaming in his direction.

"What?" he demanded when he reached the others, seeing the dead man lying in a puddle of blood outside the open doors of the bus.

"Somebody made a run for the bus—I think it was the tour guide. We got him first, then Seyyed killed him."

"So *now* what's holding him up?"

"I don't know!"

BIRKE STOOD IN THE AISLE. The gunman's robe had opened in the front and the hardware taped to his body was plainly visible. Birke knew his life was over. He had nothing left to lose. He propelled himself down the aisle and dived through the air onto the body of the gunner, who saw him only a moment before the impact and barely had time to wince. The American landed on top of him and blasted the breath out of his body.

Seyyed's gun hand was grabbed by his assailant. His other hand was trapped under the American's body. His fingers fumbled against his chest.

Birke shouted, "Pete, grab his damned hand! He's got a bomb!"

Pete moved like a rocket.

Seyyed felt the actuator beneath the material of his robe. Out the open door of the bus, across the empty, dusty ground, he spotted Eid Farid. Seyyed's lips parted in a grin of doomed triumph. He saw Farid raise his gun victoriously.

Birke felt the Egyptian's free hand moving between their bodies. Pete was trying to pull the hand away, but Birke knew he was too late. The Egyptian relaxed beneath him, wearing a smile.

For a fraction of a second Birke's world was filled with white light, then nothing.

1

The concrete office building had been gutted by fire in the distant past and was nothing more than a crude shell. An empty warehouse stood across the street, its roof cluttered with discarded trash and hulks of broken equipment. Rats scampered among the piles of garbage and were occasionally ambushed and devoured by a stealthy, wiry cat that called the roof home.

Something stepped out of the shadows and surprised even the cat, which hissed and fled, abandoning a disemboweled rodent that had been its midnight snack. The figure stood at the edge of the roof and perused the empty street.

He had evaluated the layout of the burned-out office building within seconds but remained watching, rewarded after several minutes with a hint of movement. A guard had opened the front entrance door and stepped into the night air. His automatic rifle grasped by the barrel, he peered up and down the street. There was no agitation evident in his manner, the figure on the warehouse roof noted, no sense of expectancy, nothing coming down soon, as far as the guard knew.

Nothing expected, anyway. The man on the rooftop had his own plans.

The guard retreated into the blackness, and the figure on top of the warehouse uncoiled a length of tarred hemp rope. He stepped into the open for less than three seconds and let the rope sail out of his hands. The half moon was full on his face for that moment and if anyone had been watching, he or she would have been startled. A tall white man on the roof of an old warehouse in Dailqu, Sudan, in the middle of the night in a combat blacksuit wasn't a typical sight.

The loop on the end of the rope sailed stiffly through the air and landed over the top of a wooden pole. The crossbar on the pole was bent and no longer supported telecommunications or power lines, but it still looked sturdy. The man, hidden again in the shadows, dragged on the rope, feeling the pole shift only slightly, then wrapped the rope around his wrists and stepped over the edge into the empty air.

If the guard had happened to look up in that moment he would have been even more surprised. The white man was now swooping through the air, from one side of the street to the other, then was gone from sight. The rope hung motionless between the top of the burned-out office building and the old telephone pole as if it were a permanent fixture.

MACK BOLAN WEDGED the rope in a crack in the concrete, crouched and listened for any telltale whisper of noise. There was none. In one hand he gripped the custom-silenced Beretta 93-R, his weapon of choice until the time came to make his presence known. After that, he had a number of options, all carefully situated on his person and stowed in the black backpack. He was very familiar with the placement of the gear in the pack—so familiar he could grab what he wanted without looking and without hesitation. But for now the pack went over his shoulder.

There was a burned hole gaping in the roof, allowing access to the building's interior, and the Executioner lowered himself into pitch blackness. Holding on to the jagged roof edge, he found he couldn't touch the floor with his feet. He had to risk being heard and dropped, falling only another six inches. The sound of his crepe-soled shoes impacting against the ash-covered floor sounded loud to his ears, and the soldier swept the room with the Beretta. But no one came out of the darkness after him. He couldn't assume he'd gone unheard. He was far too experienced to make such an error in judgment and was alive today because of it.

But as he stepped down the black hallway and into the stairwell, he heard nothing that indicated awareness of his presence.

There was no one inhabiting the top floor, so he descended a level. His eyes became accustomed to the near-perfect blackness, and he made out a row of bunks on the third floor. Some were inhabited and he listened to quiet snoring. Five men were sleeping there, he decided.

Bolan stepped into the room and lowered to a crouch beside the first bed. His fingers closed on a weapon—an automatic rifle, stock smooth and gleaming. In the dim moon glow he caught the glint of additional weapons near the other beds.

The sleeping man stirred and mumbled wordlessly, then grew silent again. The soldier stepped to the door, taking the gun.

If it had been warped by the fire, the door to the room might not even be functional, or it might raise enough noise to alert the sleepers to his presence. Bolan swung it and was pleased that it made no loud squeaks. When it closed, he stuck the barrel of the automatic rifle into the bottom of the door and wedged the butt against a protrusion in the broken concrete of the landing. That might hold them in for a while. Or it might do no good whatsoever.

Bolan descended another level and found what he had come looking for.

KAZEM EMAD HAD not so much a love of God as he had a hatred for mankind. All men were weak and despicable creatures. Those few who were not were to be contended with. Eid Farid was quickly becoming one of the latter.

"Congratulations on your success," he said by way of greeting. "Your plan paid off spectacularly." He spoke, however, through gritted teeth.

Farid bowed humbly. Emad breathed through his nostrils, fighting his desire to wipe the self-serving smile off the man's face with a blow to the jaw.

"We have Nabil Aman to thank for our success," Farid said. "It was his planning and persuasive powers that enabled the plan to function."

Aman was joining them from another car, which had been following minutes behind Emad's. He nodded briefly to Farid. "You did well, though you should have accounted for the bus driver. I'm surprised you didn't. Weren't you staking out the vehicles before you chose one?"

"No. We spotted a target that met our needs and utilized it."

"I hope my name is not on your lips when you're arrested for your stupidity. And you will be if you don't start thinking."

Farid glared at him. Emad fumed but said nothing. They continued in the direction of the truck, a dark silhouette in the night.

The vehicle was stopped alongside the Lake Nasser highway at the Ash-Shabb turnoff with its hood up, as if it had engine trouble, and the Sudanese truck driver was getting out to greet them.

"Open it," Emad ordered before the driver could speak.

The driver rattled his keys and found the one to open the rusty padlock on the rear door of the panel truck. He shone his flashlight inside on the stacks of wooden boxes, which were emblazoned at each end with a large, five-pointed star, heavily stylized to look like a character in the Arabic alphabet. Under the star was a company name in both English and Arabic: Star Sweet Fruit Company.

"Open them," Emad said.

The truck driver and Farid grabbed crowbars and began prying the tops off the wooden crates. Inside were masses of shredded newspapers and blankets. Farid unrolled one of the blankets and revealed a Czech Skorpion machine pistol.

Emad's eyes grew bright. "Good. Now that one."

Farid moved to one of the smaller boxes and pried at the lid, dragging off the wooden top and flinging it to the dusty desert earth. He reached into the foam niche and withdrew a block of what appeared to be white clay wrapped in plastic.

"What is it?" the driver asked.

"Plastique. Plastic explosives, my friend. And this!" Emad grabbed a bundled package of dynamite sticks. "Now we have the capability to do some real damage!"

The driver paled. "You should have told me I was carrying explosives."

"Now you know," Emad said.

He turned to Nabil Aman. "This will draw some attention, eh? We can make a noise loud enough to wake the dead!"

"Shut up, Kazem. See if you can maintain your dignity for five full minutes. We have half of what I asked for. When can we expect the rest?"

Emad was still grinning. "Driver?"

"I can go back tomorrow, same time as today. But this is dangerous, is it not, driving with explosives?"

"You made it here, didn't you?" Emad asked.

"I don't feel safe, now. They should have told me what the cargo was."

"What difference would it have made?"

"What difference? I might not have even driven it!"

Emad grabbed the man by the shirt and pulled him close. "You're not going to back out on me. You're doing God's work now! And if God wants you to bring explosives across the border, you'll do it!"

The driver was thrown to the ground.

Emad gestured grandly. "Put the explosives in my car. I want to start back to Cairo tonight. Eid, tomorrow's shipment is all yours."

"None for the other cities, Kazem?" Farid asked.

"Not yet. Aswân is ripe. And your organization has proved itself. As long as you've got the targets and the ability, the Holy Voice will speak through you. It won't take long for our targets to stop coming to this city. By then I'll have the other contingents ready." Emad smiled widely, a man on the verge of victory. "Our message won't go unheard, my friends."

THE ROOM WAS FULL of wooden crates stacked on either side, all of them bearing the logo of the Star Sweet Fruit Company. At the far end of the room was a small table where two men sat playing cards under a desk lamp and sharing a bottle of vodka, automatic weapons lying within easy reach.

Bolan stepped through the landing and descended a few more steps, far down enough to see that the bottom of the stairwell was filled with burned rubble. There had probably been an exit below at one time, but it was impassable now. The last thing the men in the room would be expecting was an attack from the rear.

The Executioner was considering his next step when he ran out of time. There was a bang from above—somebody had woken up and tried the door. A second crash was followed by profanity shouted in Arabic.

Bolan retreated into the darkness of the lower stairs and

watched the two guards come to the landing, looking up, weapons at the ready. They had a rapid conversation, then one of them started up the steps to the third floor. The soldier waited until he was out of sight, then mounted the steps. The remaining guard wheeled, startled, and made the mistake of bringing his AK-47 into play.

The Beretta spoke three times and silenced the man while his cry of alarm was still rising in his throat. He collapsed to the floor, out of the play.

Bolan mounted the landing, aiming into the storage room before he could see into it, but held his fire when no one was there. The pounding in the sleepers' room above had not yet roused interest throughout the building. He grabbed the dead man and hauled him into the blackness of the stairs, where the corpse disappeared into the rubble. The Kalashnikov followed him.

He stepped into the storage room and checked the door. It wasn't sturdy enough to buy him any time. By now he could hear conversation upstairs—the second guard had dislodged the gun, and there was an argument. Bolan hoped the sleepers were assuming one of their own had barred them in as a joke.

One of the boxes had already been pried loose, and Bolan yanked the top off, scooping at the shredded newspaper in search of the contents. His hand fell on the barrel of a weapon, and he withdrew a Heckler & Koch MP-5 A-3, with a 30-round magazine and a collapsible stock. The crate also contained an AK-47 and two AK-74 autorifles. His initial scan of the room had already told him it contained approximately forty such crates. At four weapons per crate, the room held enough hardware to outfit a small army. He closed the crate, but not before appropriating the MP-5 A-3 along with a case of the unit's 9 mm parabellum ammunition. The case went into the soldier's backpack.

The conversation on the next floor ended with muttered

curses. Bolan slung the MP-5 A-3 and stepped to the wall where he would be invisible to the returning guard. The Executioner determined by the sound of the steps that the man was returning alone, but he was also conscious that the men upstairs were now roused. He couldn't afford the slightest sound that would put them on alert sooner than absolutely necessary. He reached in his shirt and withdrew the Ka-bar fighting knife sheathed on his hip. He had whetted the anodized black blade the night before, and the edge glistened in the dim light of the storage room. The guard came through the door and halted.

"Osman?"

Bolan stepped up behind the guard so silently the man was oblivious to him until he felt the Executioner's breath on his neck. Then the steel bit into his throat, severing his vocal cords, and he sank to the floor.

The soldier stepped to the other side of the room, to a stack of small crates. He found one with a loose top and opened it, taking off the top layer of foam to reveal row after row of plastique bricks, arranged as neatly as eggs in a carton. Unwrapping a canvas-bandaged package, he found a dozen sticks of dynamite. On one end, thrown in as if in afterthought, were a few incendiary grenades. Bolan thought about taking several, then decided against the extra baggage. But he did grab the satchel of dynamite for immediate use.

He hurried to the other door, pondering the series of events that had brought him to the warehouse.

Thirty-six hours earlier Bolan, working independently, had found himself in a remote desert region of Saudi Arabia. He had been on the trail of an illegal drug shipment tied, through a complex series of barters, to a major Saudi arms dealer named Satish Malkani. The Riyadh-bound shipment of heroin had been burned, and a kilo of processed cocaine was blowing in the sands of the Arabian peninsula. Those in charge of its transport would never be heard from again.

But before expiring, they had tried to trade their lives with Intel that the Executioner found interesting: the shipment was purchased with two large caches of arms, which had been sourced through the Saudi arms dealer. Further interrogation convinced him the drivers didn't know enough about Malkani to track him. Not without some serious detective work that might take weeks on the streets in Riyadh. But he did learn the destination of the weapons—a street address in the city of Dalqu in the Sudan.

The inventory of the shipment and the address piqued Bolan's interest. He didn't think Dalqu was its final destination, and that led him to believe they would be headed to Egypt or Somalia. No good was going to come from them, of that he was certain. Now he had tracked down the second of the two shipments. If the information the drug traffickers gave him was accurate, this room contained only half the total arms and explosives. He was determined to find out more about the other half: where it had gone, what its intended purpose was and what person or organization had paid for the drugs that paid for the weaponry.

All he could see down the front steps was the outline of a closed door. Finger on the trigger of the Beretta 93-R, he descended through the darkness.

No sound or glimmer of light came from behind it. Bolan carefully placed several dynamite sticks against the wall where they would be unseen when the door was opened.

He turned the doorknob and crossed the threshold, evaluating the room he entered. There was a single desk and a desk lamp, now off, a partially boarded window with a small fan twisting in front of it, trying vainly to bring in air. Bolan headed directly for the desk. The drawers weren't locked and he rifled through them. Realistically he didn't expect Sudanese arms smugglers to keep paperwork, but there was always the possibility of finding some clue.

He found nothing worthwhile: a half-empty bottle of vodka— the same brand of cheap liquor that had been the final drink of the two guards above—and a glossy Arabic-language magazine, three months old. He tucked two more sticks of dynamite in the bottom drawer and distributed others throughout the room.

Bolan left the room, planting dynamite sticks in the empty offices along the corridor.

As he hurried to complete his task, there was a shout of anger, almost a scream, from the floor above. One of the sleepers had wandered down to the guard room. Bolan hadn't bothered to hide the second body. The puddle of gore in the middle of the floor made such a tactic pointless. The corpse was found.

Now maybe Bolan could get somewhere.

He flattened against the wall in one of the offices and listened to the exchange of words up the stairs. The other sleepers had been roused quickly and assembled in the guard room. Then the door in the hallway burst open and Bolan heard the pounding of footsteps and saw a glimmer of light. Four men raced down the hall, through the office and up the stairs, demanding to know what the commotion was.

"Search the building!" a voice bellowed. "Who's at the entrance?"

Bolan heard footsteps running back in his direction and conjured a mental picture of the approach: two men coming, one after the other. He reached the hallway just as the first sentry arrived. He grabbed him by the arm and swung him bodily, using his own momentum to direct him into the doorjamb. He cried in alarm before his skull cracked upon impact, and he crashed to the floor, his rifle spilling from his hands. By then Bolan had smashed the second man against the wall like a flattened bug, his rifle pressed uselessly between himself and the Executioner, who held his fighting knife against the man's throat.

"Where'd the first shipment go?"

The man's eyes went wide, and he muttered in strangled Arabic.

"I know you speak English. I want the destination of the first shipment of C-4. If I don't get it right now, you get your throat cut just like your friend upstairs."

"I don't know, I swear...."

Bolan exerted pressure, and the blade's well-honed edge penetrated the skin. The man felt his own blood trickling down his throat.

"I want to know names and addresses, and I want to know now."

The man was trembling by this time. "We shipped it to Egypt. We sent it to Aswân. That's all I know!"

"Who in Aswân? What's the street?"

"They'll kill me if I tell you!"

"I'll kill you if you don't."

The man was quaking with terror. Suddenly he started to scream for help. He never finished his cry. There was a gurgling noise that died with him as the blade scraped through his larynx. His last breath bubbled out of the huge wound as he flopped to the floor.

The cry hadn't gone unheard. Footsteps rattled down the stairs. Bolan snapped the MP-5 A-3 into play and targeted the door to the office. When he estimated his pursuers were about to run through, he triggered the weapon, and the loud chatter erupted through the building. The battle was begun in earnest. The spray of 9 mm parabellum rounds cut through the first hardman, who skidded on his face on the floor, while the second man fell back into the office, screaming. The soldier bounded over a corpse and into the office, where he took aim for a mercy shot. The gunman somehow saw through his world of pain and screeched, growing silent when the MP-5 A-3 ended his suffering.

There was activity up the stairs in the weapons-storage room, but now the hardmen had gathered their wits and weren't going to charge blindly into Bolan's field of fire. There was a rattle of distinctive AK-47 fire, and the tiled floor at the bottom of the stairs was ripped up by 7.62 mm rounds.

Bolan considered his options. The one voice he'd heard had suggested the front entrance wasn't guarded, at least not well. His surest bet was to make an escape quickly, before the group upstairs charged. He'd found the arms shipment he was after and chances were slim that he'd be able to get more information as to its intended destination.

He stepped almost to the line of ruined floor tile and fired up the stairs until he'd emptied the magazine on the MP-5 A-3, then jogged back toward the front entrance, inserting a fresh magazine on the way. They wouldn't come after him for at least a minute or two.

The man he'd slammed into the doorjamb was breathing, but by the severity of the damage to his skull, he wouldn't be waking soon. And he'd be dead before that. Bolan felt the reassuring weight of the several remaining sticks of dynamite in the stomach pouch of the blacksuit.

At the door at the end of the hallway, he saw another flight of stairs and a door to a lighted room standing empty at the bottom. He hastened down them, observed that the room was clear all the way to the front door, its glassless window looking out into the street. Bolan tossed the final sticks of dynamite onto the steps behind him and withdrew one of the AN-M-14 grenades from his pack. He activated the bomb and hurled it back up the stairs, into the hallway, where it rattled on the concrete. Launching himself through the empty room, he slammed through the front door and rolled to the ground even as he heard the sound of a curse from above. In the darkness he spotted a man clinging to a fire-escape ladder and another leaning out a third-floor window. They'd intended to get down to the ground and trap Bolan in the middle.

The man in the window raised his Kalashnikov, but Bolan was already triggering the MP-5 A-3, and in the next instant the grenade detonated. The man in the window absorbed the 9 mm rounds and fell from sight. The climber had been using one hand to bring his own weapon into play, and the shock of the grenade caused him to lose his grip on the ladder. He plummeted and waved his autorifle on the way down as if to ward off the approaching impact. He belly flopped on the concrete.

Bolan heard the second, more thunderous explosion rock the office building as he sprinted across the open street and into an alley. There was a chain reaction of dynamite explosions until the blasts homed in on the arms-storage room. There were screams from within as the arms traders attempted desperately to escape the approaching confrontation. But when the storage room blew, there was a sound like powerful, muffled thunder, and tongues of fire uncurled from the windows and doors. The roof flew off in small pieces, and flame belched into the night sky. The burned-out building was blazing anew.

The sky diver lying on the street was wriggling away from the fire as burning pieces of oily metal clattered around him. Bolan saw an unexpected opportunity, and there was no reason to pass it up. He jogged back into the open, eyes peeled, kicking away the crushed man's gun and flipping him on his back with his foot.

"Where in Aswân did you send the initial shipment?"

The man's clothing was surprisingly intact, but his chest was oddly caved in. Blood was pouring from his mouth, and breathing was obviously a painful effort.

"If I tell you…"

"I don't kill you. If you get to hospital anytime soon, you might even live to be an old man."

The glazed eyes saw the barrel of the H&K subgun inches away.

"Aswân…"

"I know that much. Who in Aswân? I need names." The man didn't realize he was dying. Bolan did. If only he could get another scrap of useful information first. "Where were you to drop off the shipment?"

"In the desert. Our driver scheduled to meet them tomorrow…3 a.m. Ash-Shabb turnoff."

Bolan didn't know what that meant, but he would find out.

2

The truck was burning by the side of the highway at the Ash-Shabb turnoff at 2:35 a.m.

The highway left the city of Wadi Halfa in Sudan, crossed into Egypt and traveled north parallel with the bank of Lake Nasser. The dirt road to Ash-Shabb joined it within a few yards of where the truck was burning. But no one was traveling the dirt road or the highway. The desert stretched in all directions around it, empty and unresponsive.

At 2:39 a.m. the heat reached the gas tank. The flames went momentarily white, and a heavy sound filled the night air.

At 2:57 a.m. only the canvas that had covered the rear of the truck was still burning. The rest of the vehicle sat smoking in the brilliant moonlight. The stench filled the desert for miles, but there was no one to smell it. Not a single car had passed since the truck caught fire.

At 2:58 a.m. the glow of headlights appeared from the north, slowing as the car drew closer, crawling to a halt fifty feet from the smoldering hulk. Another truck appeared and pulled up behind the car. There was no more movement for a moment, as if the occupants of the vehicle expected the burning truck to reveal its secrets if only they were patient.

There was a pop, and few orange sparks spiraled heavenward. The smoke became thinner.

Eid Farid emerged from the passenger door of the car with a pistol at the ready and a frown on his brow. He walked slowly to the truck, watching the empty horizon in all directions as if there might be something somehow hidden in the flat, empty desert. He circled the burning vehicle carefully, cautiously, ready to fire at anything suspicious. There was nothing. He waved to the others.

The car and the other truck approached and disgorged their passengers. There were now six men wandering around the burning hulk as if the blackened metal and the oily smoke might somehow yield the story of how the vehicle came to its ruinous end.

Kazem Emad kicked a bent sheet of metal that had once been the truck's side panel. "Who did this? I want to know who did this!"

"Who knew about this shipment? Who outside of our shippers and ourselves?" Farid asked. "No one."

"Someone did. Someone had to!"

"I don't think so."

"Then explain this to me!"

Farid was standing on his toes trying to see inside the truck cab. He used the material of his robe to protect his hand from the hot metal and yanked at the blackened, sprung door. The hinge, warped by heat, creaked, but the door opened partially.

"No driver," Farid observed.

Emad didn't believe him until he examined the cab himself. There was a mess of burned-out seats and controls.

"There would be some sort of remains," Farid stated.

"There's no one in there?" Nabil Aman asked from several paces away, reluctant to see for himself. "This doesn't bode well, Emad. You've got a traitor in your midst."

"You're jumping to conclusions. My men are one hundred percent devoted."

"It doesn't look like it."

"If there is a leak, it probably is on the other end, and

comes from our arms merchants. Satish Malkani must have a traitor or opportunist in his employ. Our driver fell victim to them.''

"None of our goods were in the truck when it burned. Look." Farid was standing at the rear of the truck, looking into the empty, lopsided, smoky box.

DARKNESS AND BREATHING, that was all there was to the soldier's world for a long time. He lay surrounded by the weight of the sand, cocooned in cool, heavy darkness. Another human being might have been overwhelmed by claustrophobia. Another might have felt relaxed and soothed by the cool, womblike comfort.

The Executioner was as alert as a great cat hunting for food.

There had been no place to hide. Whoever was receiving the shipment of guns and high explosives had picked the spot specifically for that purpose. The landscape was unblemished sand in all directions for miles, even the dunes too gentle to hide a man. That didn't pose a major obstacle to Bolan.

He'd scooped out a coffin-shaped impression in the earth, adding an extra cavity for his pack. He breathed through narrow plastic tubes. His other link to the surface world was one of his walkie-talkies, which he had risked leaving out in the open and turned on. The little black box was virtually unnoticeable in the night. Still, Bolan knew there was every chance it would be seen. He'd left it skewed in the sand so that, if spotted, at least it might appear to have been dropped by someone leaving the place, instead of by someone still on the scene.

He'd picked up the walkie-talkie set in Khartoum at an electronics store that catered to a wealthy clientele, paying for them with some of the cash that had almost become drug profits for the Riyadh ring. They were state-of-the-

art radios, configured at power levels that the FCC would
have frowned on in the U.S., and outfitted with specialty
headsets. Bolan had donned the headset as he covered himself in his premature grave. And he'd begun to listen.

For a long time he didn't hear anything.

Then the truck and car had arrived, stopping within a
couple yards of the radio. There were curses in Arabic as
the occupants of the truck took in the sight of the burning
truck. Bolan's luck was holding out. They believed it was
the truck that had been scheduled to meet them. They had
come from the north, as he'd assumed they would, and
had parked between himself and the fiery wreck he'd
created.

He listened to the exchange between the men, listened
to their conversation recede in the direction of the wreck.

The Executioner sat up, the sand rushing from his face,
and removed the scarf that had served to protect his eyes.
His fiery creation had become a smoky well of darkness
with occasional smoldering glimmers. The van was parked
closer to him, the car just beyond it. Both vehicles looked
empty. The figures standing around the wreckage were
oblivious to him.

The soldier rose from the ground and stalked to the van.
He had no time to cover the tracks he was making in the
sand, only to grab his spare walkie-talkie from its perch
and launch himself onto the truck.

Standing on the tailgate with one foot, he stepped on
the door handle with the other and stretched a hand to the
roof. His fingers wedged into a marginal handhold, and he
hauled himself onto the roof.

He lay flat on his back, barely moving except for one
hand freeing the Desert Eagle .44 Magnum from the backpack. For ten seconds there was silence, then he heard,
"How do we get in touch with them?"

"I don't know. They've always contacted us."

"We'll have to go through Malkani," said a gruff voice with an air of authority.

"Who knows how long it will take for this to get resolved, especially if that shipment was stolen."

Bolan heard no hint of alarm in their voices. He'd succeeded in remaining covert. He was filing away the signatures of the different voices for future reference.

"Possibly. But the Sudanese served only as agents for Malkani. He may never be able to recover the shipment."

"Then he will provide us with a replacement shipment," the gruff voice declared. "Our agreement was that the shipment be delivered to us. As far as I am concerned it belongs to Malkani until we have personally taken possession of it. And the Saudi had better agree if he wants to get any more business from us."

"Meanwhile, what about our plans for tomorrow?"

"No need to cancel. We simply alter our technique."

Bolan heard van and car doors opening and the engines started up. He turned onto his stomach as the vehicles made a wide circle and started north again on the highway. He grabbed the rim of the roof and rode out the bumps and turns. He was on the road to Aswân.

In a minute the desert was empty again, except for the dying, smoky remains of the truck.

THE LAND THEY DROVE through grew less arid, and eventually the lights of the city came into view. The truck and the car stayed together through the outlying communities feeding into Aswân, pulling off into a dark, cramped area of crumbling brick buildings and shanty houses. Bolan had remained unseen on the roof the entire trip. He stayed with them all the way to what he hoped would be their base of operation. The vehicles drove through the gates of a junk-yard full of wrecked cars and old heavy machinery. The truck maneuvered through two narrow rows of rusty scrap metal, far enough back to be invisible from the street. The car parked in the open and one of the hardmen in the front seat jumped out to close the chain-link gate and padlock it.

"We act this afternoon. We meet Malkani's man this evening. It will simply make for a full day," the agitated leader growled. Other than that, there were no comments of interest, nothing that indicated to Bolan what this group's motives might be.

He let the sounds of the men fade as they entered the three-story brick building adjacent the junkyard. He'd tracked the jackals to their den. Before he proceeded further, he wanted to know who they were, what drove them, what their intentions were.

It was time to get in touch with Stony Man.

THE LINE TOOK a full two seconds to connect, and somewhere in the United States a phone rang twice. Then there was a click that sounded as if the line were disconnected. Five more seconds passed, and the phone began to ring again. The voice that answered was rough and tired.

"Hello, Bear."

"Hal was thinking you might've fallen off the face of the earth, Striker," said Aaron "Bear" Kurtzman, resident computer expert and gatherer of intelligence at Stony Man Farm in Virginia. The Farm, unknown to most U.S. citizens, was the country's most effective weapon against terrorism.

Mack Bolan had once been closely tied to the Farm. These days he gave priority to his own endeavors, but quite often his and the Farm's agendas coincided, and Bolan wouldn't turn down Hal Brognola when the big Fed requested special assistance.

"You're lucky I was suffering from insomnia. Its 2:00 a.m. here, Striker," Kurtzman declared.

"Better put on some coffee, then. I'd like to get some Intel. There's something major going on in my neck of the woods, and I'm hoping you can tell me what."

"And what neck of the woods do you happen to be in at the moment?"

"Aswân," Bolan answered.

"I don't have to perform a data-base search to tell you what's happening in Aswân. You haven't caught a newscast in the last day or so, have you?"

"I've been otherwise involved."

"Uh-huh. There was a suicide bombing in one of the tourist centers near Abu Simbel, not far from you. The perpetrator entered a bus full of Americans and British citizens on a guided tour. There were...let's see." He swore softly. "Thirty-three people on board. All dead. Plus the bomber."

"Anybody claim responsibility?"

"Yes. A group called the Mukad'das Saut—the Holy Voice. It's one of the extremist factions in Egypt trying to eradicate the secular authority and put a Muslim government in its place."

"What do you know about this Holy Voice?"

"What can you tell me, Striker? You don't just happen to be in Aswân at the same time something like this heats up. It sounds as if you've stumbled onto them."

"It appears so. I may have foiled an attempt on their part to restock themselves with explosives and arms. And I may have found their headquarters."

"Good work. I'll see what I can dig up. Get back to me in a few hours," Kurtzman directed.

"I'll be in touch."

"Wait a second. There's something I'd like to ask you. We've heard through roundabout sources in Saudi Arabia that there's a substantial shortage of heroin on the streets of Riyadh. Seems one of the most closely guarded drug-smuggling ringleaders ended up mysteriously dead in the desert not far from Al Lith. Thought you might know something about it.''

"They were a big help. Put me on the trail of this arms shipment in the first place. I couldn't have come as far as I did without their help, and I owe them a major debt of gratitude.''

"Seems as if you paid them.''

"I did.''

Bolan hung up and walked across the street to the Ramses Monument Inn, a tourist hotel where he could get a room without being conspicuously out of place. Later on he'd procure a *galabieh* robe. Dressed like an Egyptian, and with his dark looks, he would blend in well enough on the street.

He slept six hours and had a meal, soon feeling fully restored from his exhausting efforts over the past two days. He crossed the street to the public phone and soon was patched through to Stony Man.

Aaron Kurtzman answered on the first ring. "Hello, Striker.''

"What've you got, Bear?''

"Our intelligence in Egypt isn't first-rate, but here's what I've got.'' Bolan clearly heard the tapping of a computer keyboard over the line.

"The Mukad'das Saut, or Holy Voice, was formed about a year ago by a Kazem Emad. He's from Cairo and is the son of a man named Rahman Emad, who seems to have migrated into Egypt, maybe out of Syria, and who definitely had some Shiite leanings. He nevertheless acted as *qadi* during his later years, before being ostracized for some fanatical leanings. Kazem adopted the fanaticism, though his ideology is dynamic—he joined a sect of mystic Sufis for a while, was kicked out and joined a small Kharijites group. When one of the sect leaders was found in the mosque with his skull crushed, Emad was blamed. He claimed he was innocent of the crime, but also blamed the dead man of being in league with the devil.

"He somehow managed to escape murder charges and over the next two years became increasingly extreme in his beliefs, which shifted month to month, but always included as a central theme the need to purify Egypt by making the government an Islamic government and closing off the nation to non-Muslims.

"That's the stated long-term goal of the Holy Voice. The group isn't associated with the Muslim Brotherhood, which has been in existence for decades and has been an institution aimed at peacefully changing Egypt to a Muslim nation. As far as we can tell, none of the men in the Holy Voice were ever members of the Brotherhood. And they all have pretty extensive records of violent behavior.

"The Holy Voice seemed to come into existence just after the last Organization of the Islamic Nations Conference, which was the first time the Islamic nations of the world sent a clear message that extremism and terrorism were inherently un-Islamic. Unfortunately that declaration only spurred some groups on to more extreme acts.

"Anyway, the Holy Voice's first attack occurred spontaneously, on the streets of Cairo, when Emad and his men kicked a man to death. Guess the guy's views didn't mesh with theirs. After the incident Emad claimed the man was a traitor to Islam and wanted to destroy the Muslim way of life. A lot of people believed him. A lot of people called him a hero.

"It seems Emad has now styled himself a sort of crusader for the extremist cause in Egypt. He's got his own little *jihad* going. There've been at least two more killings and several other disturbances linked to Emad and his men, and there's every indication that his ranks have been swelling. And now he's claimed responsibility for the bombing.''

Bolan was quiet, recalling the voices he had heard in the desert the night before. He'd listened to just snatches of conversation and had heard no names or organizations mentioned. While there was every indication he had stumbled onto the group, he would have to make certain.

"Hal would like to discuss this mess with you," Kurtzman said, interrupting Bolan's train of thought. "I took the liberty of letting him know what you were working on. He's had an ear glued to the phone ever since."

"Okay. Put him on."

"Just a second. There's something more I want to tell you. The Holy Voice has claimed to have Nabil Aman in its employ."

"Should that name mean something to me?"

"Not especially. He's a Palestinian, but not a member of the PLO. He's been involved in some messy situations in Israel over the years. In fact, some of the worst. Five years ago, the reports indicate, he spent some time in Iran and was trained in a kind of terrorist school. He came back with a variety of new techniques that he's used since. He's organized suicide bombings, several firebombings and has masterminded some pretty sophisticated time-bombings." Kurtzman exhaled. "This guy's responsible for a lot of innocent deaths. Both Israeli and pro-PLO."

Bolan considered this added wrinkle while he waited to be transferred. He didn't wait long.

"Striker?"

"Here, Hal."

"Aaron told me what your situation is. What are your plans from here?"

"I'm not sure yet. I don't even know for certain the arms buyers I tracked down are members of this Holy Voice. After I do, I'll determine what their situation is. I'll see how many players they've got, get an idea of their hardware inventory, try to determine what their plans are. And act accordingly. Why the interest?''

''We have a feeling this situation is going to get worse. The Holy Voice claimed that the bus bombing was only the beginning of its campaign. The group is demanding the immediate formation of a Muslim government and the arrest of all members of the current government. They're promising more deaths in the near future, and I—and others—think they mean business. But the Holy Voice has also promised to target strictly Westerners. No Egyptians. In fact, no Muslims.''

''What's the Egyptian government doing about it?''

''Investigating, naturally. But I have a feeling that some of their operations may be compromised. A large percentage of the population agrees with the Holy Voice's goals, if not its techniques. And without a direct threat to their own people…let's just say we're worried Egypt isn't trying hard enough to stop these people. This Emad may turn out to be a formidable manipulator.''

Brognola paused for Bolan's reaction but didn't get any. ''I know you're solo on this one, Striker. But I've got a request from the executive level that you go after this Holy Voice. If it is not the shoppers you tracked today then find them. Put them out of business. Otherwise, we may be looking at more American deaths.''

''Have you got other staff involved?''

''Not me. But there are Egyptian operatives at work trying to infiltrate the Holy Voice, including people who owe me favors. I can give you access to them with a few phone calls. In fact, I'd prefer it.''

''Give me one day. I'll squeeze this group and see what comes out. I'll report back, and we'll go from there.''

''Agreed.''

3

Bolan chose the small brown Audi for its lack of conspicuousness, but it was freshly washed and waxed by the rental agency and too shiny for his tastes—until he found an empty lot on the outskirts of Aswân and rubbed dirt on the car to dull the finish. Then it looked less like a rental and more like any other car that might be on the streets of Aswân for perfectly mundane reasons.

At dusk he parked at a small storefront shop and bought a thick grain porridge, slightly sweetened, for dinner. It was satisfying if bland, and he ate it as he parked on the curb and watched the street. He was almost a full block away from the junkyard building.

The food was long gone before he saw activity at the building. Three men approached and entered, then emerged with four others. The small gang started down the street on foot, crossing the road and cutting into an alley.

Bolan started the Audi and allowed it to roll at an easy pace. At an intersection prior to the junkyard, he turned to the left and cut over to the next block. The road was significantly more narrow, and he drove along it slowly, watching for pedestrians and his gang of arms buyers. They came from the alley a block ahead of him. One of the men glanced back at the car but wasn't overtly suspicious. Then the group crossed the road and entered another building.

The soldier drove past the establishment, which turned

out to be a dark, dank café, one of the many that existed on every city block in Egypt, this one definitely a place for locals.

Bolan parked and left the vehicle clothed in the Arab *galabieh,* and scarved. Underneath the robe he wore a pair of dark slacks, a black T-shirt and the leather harness for the Beretta 93-R. The robe was unbuttoned down to his stomach in the front so he could access the gun if the need arose. His dark features allowed him to pass into the night-club without any threatening looks. Those that noticed him labeled him a stranger.

He didn't hesitate about stepping across the room and sitting at a low table within a couple paces of the group he was trailing, which he'd spotted upon entering. The men were leaning together across their own table, a ceramic bowl of sugar serving as the hub to their conversation.

Of which there was little, as yet. They'd come to meet with the local agent of the arms dealer Satish Malkani. There was an occasional comment, some gruff, humorless laughter. He got the impression they were men waiting to get bad news.

A young man stepped to the edge of his table. "Tea," Bolan said in Arabic. The waiter displayed no suspicion and Bolan's accent, if not perfect, was passable. For the time being. The tea appeared in a minute.

He sensed one of the men at the other table eyeing him, and he glanced at his watch, then toward the door, and the man at the other table looked away. Bolan was so far conveying the image of a man waiting to meet someone who was late for the appointment, but not seriously so. He added several spoonfuls of sugar to the tea to keep up appearances and sipped it, then noticed a pair of men entering the dimly lit establishment. They stood by the door, eyes passing from table to table. One of the men looked frankly at Bolan, who met the gaze only long enough to appear disinterested. The table of seven from the junkyard became silent, and one man gestured to the two by the door, who came to them cautiously.

"Eid," said the newcomer, with a haggard, unkempt shock of dark hair, "the news I bring is not good."

"Sit down, Gamal."

"We have heard news from Sudan. From Dalqu. There was an explosion."

"Not the plastique?" Farid asked.

"I am afraid it was all destroyed. All it took was for one of the grenades to go off. Then, of course, the entire place went up. None of the Sudanese shippers survived."

Eid Farid was contemplating this when one of his companions spoke up. "Then who drove the truck to the meeting spot?"

Gamal made an empty movement with his hands. "Who knows? But it was not the dealers' truck. Theirs was garaged at the site and was destroyed in the fire the night before the rendezvous took place—or was scheduled to."

"Then why was a truck there?" Farid demanded.

"I don't know," said the wild-haired man. "Maybe it was just a coincidence that it was in the right spot—"

"Coincidence? Bah!" Farid glowered. "In the exact spot of the meeting? It was set up for us to find. Or the story is a lie."

"A lie?" Gamal asked. "It is very doubtful they could have found another buyer for the shipment. What purpose would there have been for such a lie?"

"I don't know. Yet." Farid was frowning and staring into space. Bolan felt his eyes on him, and he looked at his watch again. Farid looked away.

"Could someone be on our trail?" one of Farid's men asked.

"How could there be?" another asked.

"What concerns me is the matter of the truck at the meeting spot," Farid said. "That was no coincidence and no accident. Someone wanted us to find a truck where and when we were scheduled to find it."

"But to what end? I could see it if they were planning to attack us there. But there was no one even in the vicinity when we were there."

"That we saw," Farid muttered.

"You chose that location because it was immune to surprise attack," Gamal reminded Farid. "If there'd been anybody there, we would have seen him."

Farid didn't respond.

Bolan risked a glance sideways, pretending he was looking to the window, and noticed Farid was again looking at him. If he was suspicious of the soldier, the emotion didn't yet register on his grim face. Maybe he was only staring at a stranger in what was obviously an establishment for local clientele.

"What does Malkani intend to do?" Farid asked.

Gamal looked uncomfortable. "He has not yet said. He is searching for more plastique...."

There was a quiet drumbeat from a small speaker hanging near the ceiling, then a raspy tune from a well-worn record began to play. A ceiling light shone on a stage smaller than one of the tabletops, onto which an Egyptian woman stepped. She might easily have been attractive once, in her revealing, ornamented dancer's outfit. Now her face showed the blank emotion of one who had performed the same routine a thousand times and was no longer inspired. She began to move with a studied languidness to the music, utterly devoid of passion.

Bolan couldn't hear the conversation at the neighboring table over the music and knew he'd be pressing his luck if he stayed until after the performance. He rose, tossed three silver coins on the table and exited unhurriedly.

The street was quieter than it had been. The sky was clear, but the moon was hidden behind the buildings, which made the city very dim at street level. There were no streetlights. Bolan stepped to his rental car and slid behind the wheel. No one followed him from the nightclub.

But his subterfuge had gained him next to nothing.

He had sat in the car for less than three minutes when his attention was drawn to two men walking down the narrow street carrying a large box. Even in the dark he made out the familiar legend of the Star Sweet Fruit Company.

Bolan ducked low as the men walked by the Audi, and in the rearview mirror he watched them meet with the group from the café at the same instant a small convertible pulled to a stop. The box was loaded into the back seat of the vehicle, and two of the men climbed into it. The convertible pulled away and left Farid and the rest of the men behind.

Another car, an old station wagon, turned onto the street and stopped just long enough for Farid and the rest of his group to pile inside. They pulled past Bolan, and a quick glance told him Farid was watching the Audi from the window as he drove by.

Bolan put the vehicle in gear and drove after them.

The convertible and the station wagon traveled quickly to the highway and headed south, out of Aswân. As the dark closed in, so could Bolan, moving in tight behind the other vehicles, his headlights making it impossible for his quarry to identify the car. Weaving in and out of traffic made it tough for the drivers to keep an eye on him, if they were even wary of potential pursuit.

It soon became clear that the occupants of the convertible and the station wagon were watching for a vehicle coming from the opposite direction. And Bolan grew cold when he realized it was a bus they were searching for. Each time the shape of a bus could be seen ahead in the northbound lanes the two cars pulled to the inside median and slowed. Bolan was forced to do the same. The bus would pass by the two vehicles, and they would speed up again.

Then the occupants of the cars identified their target. Bolan, watching the behavior of the convertible and the station wagon, pinpointed the moment the decision was made. Both cars slammed on their brakes, swerved into the median and came to a full stop.

By that time the bus was passing Bolan, and he glimpsed the words Desert Tours painted in large blue letters on the side—another bus full of tourists, returning to their Aswân hotels after a day spent at the Abu Simbel monuments.

The convertible and the station wagon waited for a small gap in the traffic and shot out into the northbound lanes, accelerating rapidly and shooting past Bolan's Audi.

The soldier waited until they disappeared from his rearview mirror, then slammed on the Audi's brakes, wrenching the wheel and sliding sideways in a cloud of dust. In a moment he was tearing into the northbound lane after them.

The Audi wasn't an ideal high-performance vehicle, but Bolan coaxed it to top speed and soon found himself maneuvering through the light traffic. Within minutes he spotted the station wagon, proceeding at a steady rate three lengths behind the Desert Tours bus.

The convertible was nowhere to be seen.

Bolan accelerated around the station wagon, then spotted the convertible a few lengths in front of the bus, keeping pace. He could see figures in the rear seat working busily and realized they were prepping their weapons.

In that instant the convertible driver gestured ahead. The

back seat figures looked up, and Bolan followed their gaze. In that instant their plan became all too clear.

The ground was rocky, and leading to a bridge over a sudden drop-off. The chasm was wide and of indeterminate depth. The gunners planned to take out the bus driver, maybe the tires, and send the vehicle out of control and careening into the chasm.

The crash would kill the occupants of the bus just as effectively as any bomb.

Bolan stepped on the gas pedal, and the Audi's small engine whined to higher revs, pushing to greater speeds than the bus and the convertible. He came alongside the bus, and in that moment watched the station wagon jet out from behind the vehicle into his rearview mirror. It closed fast.

The Executioner had the big Desert Eagle on the seat beside him and coaxed more speed out of the Audi, homing in on the convertible, and the automatic weapons he had been expecting made their appearance. The two men in the back seat were talking quickly and pointing at him.

Bolan took the initiative, raising the big .44 Magnum handgun, holding it out his window and leveling it at the driver of the convertible. He triggered a round, but at the same moment the station wagon crashed into the rear of the Audi, sending the shot wild. The convertible driver ducked and craned his neck.

The gunmen in the rear of the convertible took their targets. And one was the Executioner. He yanked on the wheel, swerving the Audi, and the sound of automatic-rifle fire was followed by the crash of glass from his passenger-side window. The other gunner was targeting the bus driver, and Bolan swerved back in the convertible's direction. The station wagon was homing in on his back end again, but he raised the Desert Eagle and fired before the next impact. The .44 round crashed into the skull of the gunner.

The bus was swerving and slowing and Bolan had no way of knowing if he'd saved the driver. The second impact of the station wagon shivered through the Audi, but Bolan steered with the crash and directed his vehicle into the rear of the convertible, flooring the gas pedal for even more speed. The nose of the Audi crunched into the rear of the convertible, eliciting a look of surprise from the second gunner, who didn't take the clean, open shot at Bolan in the fraction of a second he had the opportunity.

The soldier wasn't the kind of man to let such a chance pass by. In the moment the two vehicles were in intimate contact, he sighted and fired the Desert Eagle. Milliseconds later the second gunman looked down at the ruin of his chest, then flopped sideways onto the seat.

The bus was falling behind, pulling to the side of the road. Bolan swerved into the middle of the highway again, braced himself and rode out the third impact from the station wagon, swerving suddenly to avoid a volley of autofire from behind.

The convertible's driver was looking over his shoulder as if unable to believe both his passengers were dead, then he looked to the other side and spotted the Executioner closing in. He swerved away, and his tires bit into the rocky shoulder of the highway. Bolan fired again, the big .44 round chewing a large chunk of flesh from the driver's shoulder. The convertible lurched off the road and launched itself into the chasm.

Bolan didn't wait to hear the imminent impact. He wrestled the Audi into a spin, stomping on the brake, and created quadruple clouds of acrid smoke from the overheated tires. The vehicle traveled sideways for several seconds, then completed rotating, facing the way it had come. Bolan wrestled the vehicle one-handed for control and raised the Desert Eagle again.

The station wagon was screeching to a halt in a desperate attempt to avoid crashing into the Audi, and Bolan watched the driver's shock as he found himself face-to-face with the big handgun. He twisted the wheel, bringing the car into its own spin, and his quick thinking saved his life. The blasts from the .44 Magnum crunched into the body panels and windows of the station wagon as it screeched to a halt and accelerated away from the Audi.

The vehicle had stalled. Bolan started it but found it sluggish, and watched the station wagon make its escape.

The tourist bus was sitting off the side of the road, windshield intact, driver and passengers apparently unhurt. The killers had been foiled.

Bolan had failed to notice the loud explosion of the plummeting convertible, but the flickering light from the flames was now visible. That, the warrior thought, was some satisfaction.

But he didn't yet have hard evidence that this group was the Holy Voice.

It was time for a little break and enter.

IT TOOK ONLY a couple of minutes to bring the Audi back to life and head back into Aswân. Within twenty minutes he arrived at the junkyard building, which now showed evidence of habitation. There were lights in the lower two levels, and signs of movement were visible but Bolan saw no guard.

He was counting on a cushion of at least fifteen minutes before the occupants of the station wagon braved a return to the city.

Bolan parked around the corner, stripped out of the robe and approached on foot. As he came to the junkyard, he scanned up and down the street, spotted no one, then proceeded into the darkness of the yard. Immediately he was surrounded by the piles of debris, mostly battered automobiles and remnants of heavy machinery. Parked among the junk were the vehicles that had been used for the desert drive very early that morning.

He mounted the rear stairs, which he'd seen used the night before. The door was locked and solid, and he couldn't risk breaking in that way for fear he would be heard and seen. The soldier was counting on getting in and out without witnesses.

The windows on the second floor were without glass, and the shutters stood open to allow in the breeze. There was his way in. He stepped carefully onto the decaying remains of a pickup truck, then maneuvered from the roof of the vehicle to a narrow ledge in the brickwork over the door. Grabbing the open window ledge above him he hauled himself up.

Hanging like a fly on the side of the building, he established that the room was empty, then crawled inside. He found himself in a bedroom, with a messy bed and a low chest. Leaving the room, he moved down the hall, stopping at several doors, finding unoccupied bedrooms. At the stairs he listened to the activity and conversation among the women of the house on the floor below. No sound came from the floor above.

Bolan ascended and found a single large sitting room, laid out with low, comfortable futons and pillows, and a large, low dining table. A telephone with a tapeless answering mechanism sat on the table, red lights glowing. When and if the group held meetings in the building, it would be in this room.

He stepped to the table and quickly removed one of his walkie-talkies and a roll of black tape—wide, with a strong adhesive. He turned on the device, adjusting it to send only. He should get several hours of full-strength battery life out of it. Then he secured it under the wooden table, directly in the center, where it was least likely to be discovered. He randomly picked a few of the futons and reclined on them, assuring himself the communications device wouldn't inadvertently be spotted by anyone in the room under normal circumstances.

All the while he was listening closely to the murmurs of conversation from the first floor. The women sounded as if they were involved in simple domestic tasks, probably preparing the evening meal. That changed suddenly. There was a greeting in Arabic, the close of a door, then heavy footsteps on the stairs.

Bolan snatched his backpack from the table and stepped across the room to the doorway, where he flattened against the wall and listened, the silenced Beretta 93-R poised against his chest. Two men came up. They stepped into the room, and the Executioner, as silent as a shadow, slipped out behind them.

He descended only four steps before there was a movement below him; another man was coming up the stairs. The new arrival shouted abruptly, grabbing inside his robe. Bolan waited until he saw the barrel of a pistol emerging, then fired quickly twice. The suppressed shots drilled into the gunman's chest and throat. He gasped and toppled backward.

There was a rush of bodies above him, and Bolan swiveled, leveling the Beretta at the doorway. He didn't wait for the gunner to bring his own handgun into play. He fired once, staggering the man, while the second mangler drilled a hole in his forehead. He collapsed to the floor.

Bolan fired into the ceiling, just enough to convince the remaining gunman he was still on his toes, then continued his descent to the second level. Another male figure burst through the screams coming from the first floor into the stairwell and stopped short when he spotted Bolan. He

peered into the darkness and shouted in Arabic, bringing
a weapon to bear in the darkness. The soldier punctuated
the remark with two more shots from the Beretta. The
gunman's shoulders shrugged, and he fell sideways.

Hearing more male voices mixed with the screaming
below, Bolan stepped into the hallway and raced to the
back bedroom, to his window entrance. A glance outside
showed the junkyard still dark and empty. He stepped onto
the sill and pounced to the top of the pickup truck. The
metal caved in eight inches, and Bolan leaped again to the
ground, tucking and rolling over and up, then bounding
behind the nearest mountain of junk.

He glanced back to the window, which was still empty.
They might not yet even know he'd left the premises.
They'd map his exit easily enough, however. He couldn't
afford to stay in the vicinity. Ducking through the piles of
metal, he found his way to the street and to the parked
Audi.

4

Bolan watched for pursuit, but none came. He flipped the other walkie-talkie to receive. Sounds of chaos rushed out of the tiny speaker. He knew enough Arabic to make out the gist of the conversation—mostly rhetorical demands for the identity of the intruder. There was an order for the women to come up and remove the bodies of the slain men, and when they arrived their wailing laments were shrill. Apparently one of the dead men was husband to one of the women and was related to most of the other men. Bolan could have guessed that the group was largely familial.

Then he heard new arrivals on the scene.

"What happened here?" the man named Eid Farid asked.

Several of his men began to explain the battle simultaneously: how the intruder had been in the sitting room when they arrived and had slipped out behind them; how he might have slipped out entirely unnoticed if Musa hadn't been coming up the stairs thirty seconds behind them; how he was a white man, clean shaved, dark complected, in black clothing. Farid demanded details about the man's appearance but was dissatisfied with the answers.

"Do you know who it was, Eid?"

"We saw that man earlier tonight," Farid said. "He was

the man in the café and he was the man who killed our brothers.''

Another man wondered what connection the intruder might have had to the burned-out truck and the destroyed arms shipment.

"I was thinking along those lines myself. We might have drawn too much attention. I think we need to call for instructions."

There was a general hush in the room when Farid got on the phone. Then he said the name Bolan had been waiting to hear.

"I need to speak to Kazem Emad."

Positive ID. Bolan now knew he was on the trail of the Holy Voice.

Farid waited a moment, obviously listening for his leader's voice on the end of the line. Then he said, "Kazem, we've had a situation develop."

Farid offered his explanation—of the man in the café, the failure of the bus attack and the infiltration of the home base. Then he waited in silence.

"What about tomorrow?" Farid asked. He listened to his orders. "Do you think that is the wisest plan? It will be a major risk to all of us!"

After listening a moment, Farid apologized, then hung up.

There was a silence. One of the others ventured, "Are our plans for tomorrow proceeding, Eid?"

"Yes, they are proceeding. Both our strikes are proceeding. Tomorrow. Simultaneously."

His men expressed amazement and doubt. "Making both strikes at once will be dangerous, Farid. We'll be stretched too thin. If we meet resistance, there might be trouble."

"Yes..." Farid clearly had his own opinion of the matter, but thought better of expressing it. "It can't be helped.

Kazem has given the order and he knows best. We proceed with the plan as we have outlined it before. We will split up now. You will receive your targets when you call him in the morning.''

His voice lowered. "Code word for Strike Force One is 'purity.'" Farid's next words were drowned out by a passing car. "Remember, tonight no more than three to a group and no two groups are to contact one another or be within a kilometer of one another until we meet on-site in the morning. We proceed with or without all the groups assembled. If one group is apprehended, then the rest go without them. We will not be stopped! Our will is greater than the will of the enemies! We fight to make Egypt God's nation! Now go!"

Bolan watched out the rear window of the Audi. The men left from the junkyard building and scattered in all directions, disappearing like rats into the alleys.

The contingent's strategy was well conceived. As it stood, Bolan could do nothing until the next day to stop them, when their orders came in and they knew where they would be striking. His predicament was complicated by the fact they planned on striking two targets at once, and as good as he was, he couldn't be two places at one time.

Bolan knew when it was time to call in reinforcements.

"WAIT A MOMENT," Kazem Emad said, and pushed the Mute button on the telephone. The red LED glowed. Nabil Aman, lounging on the couch nearby, leaned forward, elbows on knees.

"They've picked up a tail," Emad admitted. "He stopped them cold on the highway and he raided their headquarters in Aswân, though there was nothing incriminating for him to find. And they surprised him in the middle of the burglary. He killed a few of their men."

"This is the party they feel is responsible for the burning truck in the desert?'' Aman asked, then shook his head before Emad could answer. ''This man came from the south, from the Sudan. He caught on to them via the dealers who were shipping us the arms from Malkani. He destroyed their base and our goods, and found out from them where they were planning on meeting us in the desert outside Abu Simbel. He staged the burning truck as a diversion, then planted a tracking device on our vehicles while they were stopped. Maybe he even hitched a ride with us. However it was accomplished, they very effectively exposed themselves to this enemy.''

Emad waved the phone. ''So what do we do?''

''They are planning their second strike tomorrow and the third in three days.''

''Yes.''

''They will make both strikes tomorrow instead. The weakest among them will be caught or killed. The strong members—if there are any—will survive long enough to join us here in Cairo, and that will be a sign they are fit to remain members of our Holy Voice. The others will simply be lost to us. But let them act tomorrow and accomplish what they may.''

''I won't just write them off,'' Emad growled. ''I've known some of them for years. They've proved their loyalty to me. I'm honor bound to be loyal to them.''

''You're bound to serve your purpose—to make Egypt God's nation. You've told me that often enough. Sometimes prices must be paid. Sacrifices made. Make this sacrifice or weaken your army's overall strength.''

Emad scowled and with the press of a button, the LED on the phone died. ''Eid.'' He paused. ''Yes. Tomorrow you make both the strikes we have been preparing for—you make two strikes at one time.''

Farid tried to argue the point. He pointed out that, without the back-up they required at each operation, the risks were substantially increased. His argument was wise, and Emad had no opposing rationale he felt comfortable spouting. "That is what has been decided at the highest levels of the Holy Voice, Eid. This is the plan you will carry out."

Farid was chastised if not convinced. Emad reminded him of the need to stay separated until the time to strike. Several targets could never be rounded up. As dangerously exposed as they apparently were, they had to sprinkle themselves about the city. It had to be impossible for an opposing agency, whatever its source, to strike them all down or swoop them all up.

Then he hung up the phone and glared at Nabil Aman. "I won't abandon them. Any that survive I will retrieve."

"Do as you think best. Right now we cannot concern ourselves with them. We have other plans to make."

"Such as?"

"It is now clear that our second shipment will not be forthcoming from the Sudanese. We have more than enough in terms of arms to keep our men active. However, we are short on plastique. Who knows how long before Malkani can replace that shipment? We have to reengineer our plans if we are going to maintain the ferocity of our attacks—and keep the name Holy Voice at the forefront of the minds of the world's leaders."

Emad tapped the arm of his chair and considered the words. He couldn't be suspicious of Aman's strategies. They were sound, ruthless and full of cunning. Aman was nothing if not skilled in methods of terror. "Very well. How can we change our plans to maximize our resources?"

"Bigger targets," Aman said simply.

BOLAN WAS ON THE PHONE to Hal Brognola within fifteen minutes of the dispersal of the junkyard terrorists.

"Your guess was on target," he said. "It is the Holy Voice—or at least its Aswân contingent." He explained his foray into their realm and what he'd gathered from the overheard phone conversation.

"So they've got two more acts of terrorism up their sleeve in the Aswân area alone, and both are due to come down tomorrow at the same time. They are instructed to carry out the plan no matter what. I could track down a few of them in one night, but there's no way I could guarantee to get all or even most of them. And none of them even know the source of tomorrow's attack. That information will come to them from Emad in the morning, and who knows where he is."

"It's a hell of a fix," Brognola agreed, frustration in his voice. "You're right. You're going to need extra firepower backing you up on this one."

"What have you got available?"

Brognola shuffled papers. "We've got Salah Abi. He's commander of a special agency of Egypt's own antiterrorist task force, under authority of the General Directorate for State Security Investigations, or GDSSI, and moved into Aswân in the last thirty-six hours. He's got about ten men under his direct command. I know for a fact he's got few leads in his own Holy Voice investigation. I've called in a couple of favors, and he's received orders to cooperate. He'll be willing to help, especially once you start feeding him the information you've acquired so far."

"Where's his HQ?"

Brognola read an address and Bolan identified it quickly as a street not far from his locale. "He's on duty tonight," Brognola added. "He'll be expecting you."

THE BRICK BUILDING just off Sheikh Marsafy Street was well lit but quiet, and the uniformed man at the desk, intent on his paperwork, jumped to his feet when he suddenly realized there was dark figure standing before him.

"Salah Abi."

"One moment." The man went to find his commander.

A moment later Bolan was ushered into a sparse, utilitarian office with a creaking rattan ceiling fan. Proffering a hand was a powerful barrel of a man with a bushy mustache and an easy smile.

"Mike Belasko! Good to meet you."

"Salah Abi."

"I have been talking briefly with your friend. You come recommended, Mr. Belasko, and I understand you may have achieved some success where I have been unable."

"Can we talk here?"

Abi shook his head and grabbed a set of keys from the desk, turning off the floor lamp. He spoke briefly to the man at the desk, then he and Bolan left the building together.

"Let's take a drive," Abi suggested, ushering the soldier to a police squad car.

The vehicle passed through dark, quiet streets, with only the occasional dwelling showing a light.

"Peaceful enough to look at, eh? These murderers come to violate my peace. And they perform their violent deeds in the name of God—fah!"

"And it looks like they may be performing more very soon. Like tomorrow."

"Yes. So Mr. Brognola led me to believe. I wasn't too happy when I was told I needed to let you in on my investigation. Then I learned you were already tracking some members of the Holy Voice—I can't argue with success. We must prevent more terror from happening. We must stop these men from killing again. What have you learned, Mr. Belasko?"

"Very little that's useful, unfortunately. I tracked down

an Aswân cell of the Holy Voice. These are the men responsible for the suicide bombing in Abu Simbel. I know where they're based.''

Abi stamped on the brake and yanked the car to the curb. "You know where they are! You should have told me at once! We'll get a team and go get them this minute."

"No good. They've split up. They got their orders and scattered throughout the city. They've been commanded by their leader, a local named Eid Farid, to break into small groups and proceed with their attacks tomorrow, even if some of them are seized. There may be a few members staying at the base I discovered, but for the most part I think only a single family resides there. After my probe this afternoon, they may very well have moved everyone out.''

"You went in there alone?" Abi gave him a sidelong glance that indicated he thought Bolan might have a death wish. "I think you better tell me all you know, and we can go from there, Mr. Belasko."

Bolan agreed and proceeded with the story. He didn't bother telling Abi how he came to find the base for the Aswân Holy Voice. That was information the man didn't need to know. But he gave him a full accounting of the conversation between Eid Farid and Kazem Emad.

"Now," the soldier said when he'd finished, "how many men can you get on the streets by tomorrow afternoon."

"We could have every police officer in Aswân alerted."

"And how effectively can they cover all the tourist spots in the area?"

Abi shrugged, and his expression was helpless. "Like every police force in the world, we are faced with a limited budget. It's never as fully staffed as it should be, and I have a personal force of just ten."

"We'll have to make do. It's a bad idea to alert the police that we expect an attack tomorrow in case the Holy Voice has members in the ranks. Can you stress the need for extra vigilance, maybe extra men on the streets tomorrow without tipping off what we know?"

"I'm tight with many high-level police in this city. I can do it," Abi said. "Do you have any knowledge that there are terrorists among the police?"

"It's just a possibility. Your country does have its share of radicals in all levels of bureaucracy, just as every government does."

The man nodded. "We'll do it."

"But a few extra cops is still a flimsy safety net. Let's divide your men into two mobile forces."

"For what purpose?"

"I'm going to spend the rest of the night making inquiries. When and if I find out where the attacks will take place, I want your men ready to respond. You and I will stay in radio contact as much as possible."

"But what can I do in the meantime?"

"Outside of mobilizing your troops, I'm afraid nothing. Just sit tight until tomorrow morning."

"Sitting tight doesn't sit well with me, Mr. Belasko."

"I know how you feel."

BOLAN WAS HOPING that some members of the Holy Voice had remained behind at its base of operations, but doubted Farid was stupid enough to allow such a thing. He parked the Audi and stalked through the quiet darkness of the junkyard once again, and a minute later found himself entering into the building for the second time in six hours.

This time he entered via the front door. Five minutes of silence assured him there was no one moving around on the bottom floor, and he picked the simple lock with minimal noise. He stepped into the building boldly, the suppressed Beretta 93-R in hand.

He'd half expected to find the place stripped and deserted. Instead, the doors to the bedrooms on the first and second floors were mostly closed, and through them he heard the deep breathing of sleepers. One door had been left open, and inside he observed a woman slumbering on a large, low bed with two children. The Holy Voice had left their families behind, confident no harm would come to them. Bolan knew the men had revealed nothing to these women and children that would be of any use should the police interrogate them.

Assured there were no members of the terrorist group on-site, the Executioner ascended to the conference room on the third floor. None of the furnishings had been removed. Maybe the Holy Voice was so full of confidence it planned to return here after weeding out the man who had tracked them down. The walkie-talkie he'd taped under the table was still in place, and he retrieved it. That wasn't all he took.

This time the house had remained peaceful throughout his visit. He made his way down the stairs silently, left the building and returned to the Audi. Not a single sleeper in the house had been disturbed, and Bolan had what he had come for.

5

At 9:00 a.m., in Salah Abi's office, Bolan plugged in the electronic telephone-answering device he had taken from the headquarters of the Holy Voice. He then hit the Redial button. The tape recorder on the desk was plugged into the handset through a Lanier telephone coupling device and would clearly record each tone as it was automatically dialed. The number could then be deciphered by matching the tones to the numbers.

He dialed the number twice and both times received a busy signal, a good sign that he was on the right track. The various groups were calling in for their instructions. Bolan wasn't at all certain that Kazem Emad was the last person Eid Farid had dialed, and he wasn't at all certain that 9:00 a.m. was the time arranged for the members of the Holy Voice to call to learn the targets of their strikes.

The third time he got a single ring, and the phone was picked up halfway through it. There was no greeting, but Bolan heard someone breathing.

He spoke the Arabic word for *purity*.

"Archaeological museum." Then the line went dead.

"How many archaeology museums are there in Aswân?" Bolan asked.

"Just the one of any size, on Elephantine Island."

"That's one target."

Abi smiled broadly. "We have somewhere to start, at least. Without this we would have nothing."

Bolan agreed. But a half-successful day would still mean a lot of dead innocent people.

THE ASWÂN ARCHAEOLOGICAL Museum lay on Elephantine Island in the Nile, along with reconstructed Nubian villages and other tourist attractions. Ferries carried sightseers from shore to island and back again, a pleasant afternoon of cultural sights, a more relaxing and easy follow-up to a day spent walking around the statues at Abu Simbel.

Lauren Purie was doing just that. The extended bus rides and long walks—not to mention the tension—had been too much for her mother, who had opted out of the Elephantine Island trip. She'd told Lauren to go ahead without her. She would spend the afternoon relaxing with her book and watching the people from the balcony of her hotel room.

The young woman watched the Nile during the ferry ride over. The day was crisp and clear, and the river was spectacularly dotted with wooden barges, so similar to the utility barges that had traversed these very waters in Ramses's day. The previous day she had been dumbfounded by the statues of the famous pharaoh.

She'd heard there was a limited collection of artifacts in the Aswân museum, but there was little else to see in the city itself. And she was determined to make the most of every minute.

She and her mother had both been very worried after the tourist attack of several days earlier, but security had been stepped up. The police were everywhere in Abu Simbel. And they had paid and planned for this trip for months. In the end they had decided to take their chances.

But her heart nearly stopped in her chest when she stepped off the ferry and was confronted by a man with a machine gun.

BOLAN TOOK IT UPON himself to reassure the tourists on the boat. He and Abi had been unable to communicate with the ferry services until this particular craft was on its way to the island. In fact, they quickly realized keeping all the tourists from the area was a logistical impossibility short of making a public announcement, which would probably do more harm than good.

"Quiet, please," he said in a normal tone. "We have a potentially dangerous situation on the island. We're going to put you in a saferoom until we feel we've got everything under control."

Immediately there were demands for an explanation. Bolan ignored them. "Follow that officer." He indicated one of Salah Abi's men.

"Why can't we just take the ferry back?" demanded an American in a bright red-and-yellow tropical shirt.

"Because there's a chance it is rigged with explosives," Bolan said. The group quietly set out with the police officer in the direction of the museum, where a storage room had been set aside for their safekeeping. Bolan and several guards watched the group carefully along their route, following at a distance. Once they had made it to the storage room, the Executioner entered behind them. Five of Salah Abi's guards were with him.

"Now, if these men might borrow some of your clothing…"

FARID SAT ON THE STERN of a barge, watching Elephantine Island through his binoculars. There were a few wandering Americans within sight. Nothing out of the ordinary.

He turned his lenses to the other craft on the Nile. Almost imperceptibly several vessels were drifting in the direction of the island, as if drawn there by lazy currents. A few small wooden barges, a couple of motorboats. Even a man on a Jet Ski, zooming around in crazy circles, seemed to be getting closer to the island's shore, moving into position. The waiting was almost ended. Everything was shifting into place, and Farid was pleased.

As the boat came to the dock, he stepped from the barge, along with his two closest lieutenants, his Ingram submachine gun invisible under his robe.

He glanced down the shore, where six craft had now landed. Even the man on the Jet Ski had beached it and was walking along the sand. They were Farid's troops, and he was proud of the precision with which the plan was being carried out.

The two motorboats pulled away from the dock after dropping off several men and would come to shore and serve as getaway craft. The barges had been purchased cheaply and would be abandoned.

Some of the men were heading to the front of the building. Others were going in via an employee-only side door that they knew wouldn't be locked. Farid and his two accomplices entered the rear of the museum, withdrawing their weapons from beneath their robes.

They strode through the rear hallway, past the empty museum offices. Farid had no wish to take unnecessary lives—Egyptian, Muslim lives. They came to the door to the public areas and looked through. There was a disappointing lack of patronage. Maybe five or six tourists milling about the place, three cloistered at the display of a skull mutilated during some ancient ceremony. Farid would have much preferred a large tour group.

No matter. The deaths of these men would send an effective message to the world.

Suddenly it occurred to Farid that all the tourists were men, which struck him as odd. In the fraction of a second before his mind made the leap to the possibility that they had entered a trap, he heard movement behind him— movement from the supposedly empty office.

"Freeze! Drop the weapons."

Out of the corner of his eye, Farid glimpsed the familiar uniform of the Aswân police. But he knew that the man holding the police pistol hadn't been training with anywhere near the intensity Farid had been training in recent months. The terrorist moved efficiently, bringing the Ingram to chest level and loosing a burst. The officer looked surprised as five .45-caliber rounds cut into his chest and stomach. Another police officer dived for cover in one of the doorways.

Farid swiveled and kicked open the door to the public area, triggering the subgun and rattling off rounds—then stopped short. The tourists were suddenly gone. A fraction of a second later he glimpsed movement behind a trash can, and a shot was fired. His slow-acting lieutenant gagged on the slug that drilled into his mouth, and crumpled. Farid blasted the trash can, then swept the room, spotting other figures crouched in hiding behind protective barriers and displays. They had walked into a trap!

He launched himself sideways as a figure emerged from behind a display, where Farid hadn't spotted him. The man had the advantage of milliseconds, and the terrorist dived to the ground behind a case containing fragments of a gilt sarcophagus. He watched helplessly as his remaining companion took three slugs in the gut and slammed against the door. Farid cursed and peered around the display, but now couldn't even see the enemy who had shot his friend. He swept autofire across the room again, just to keep the other gunman humbled, and in the quiet that followed he listened to muffled gunfire from other parts of the museum—single rounds, guns he knew didn't belong to his men. The trap was spread throughout the museum. Their message would never be sent!

But their efforts weren't in vain. This was but part one. Part two of this day's activity was even now under way.

Just because the police somehow knew of this attack didn't mean they knew of the second attack. Especially if they had gotten their intelligence before the previous evening; only last evening had the second attack been scheduled.

That would be something. There would still be a message sent to the world.

Farid could do nothing more here. There were no tourists to kill. Just police. And the killing of police might even be hushed by the government. There would be no message sent at all.

He stood quickly and laid a suppressing fire across the room before bolting. He jumped the corpses that had been his companions and crashed through the door, into the rear hallway, triggering his weapon to clear the path. He was picturing the landscape at the rear of the museum. He would break out the back door at a full run, protecting himself all the way with a constant stream of fire. He would run for the dock, wave in a speedboat and make his escape. The others...God would save them or take them.

A cop recoiled from Farid's blazing Ingram, flopping behind a desk. Then the terrorist reached the end of the hall and shouldered the door, bursting onto the concrete platform.

He saw a man in black with a handgun, waiting for him. Farid could almost see the burst of 9 mm rounds coming at him. They ripped into his right knee, and he fell down the steps to the ground, screaming.

"Where's the other attack?" Bolan's quiet, commanding words cut through the screams of the wounded man. He looked up and saw the barrel of the Beretta 93-R directed at his chest.

"I won't ask again. Where's the second attack taking place?"

"Fuck you," Farid growled. Then he poured the rending pain and his intense anger into one desperate act—he brought his Ingram subgun out from under him. He never had time to raise it. There was a triple blast from the Beretta, and Farid's heart was cut to pieces inside his body as if with the murderous intent of a skilled surgeon.

Salah Abi rounded the corner a moment later with a handcuffed terrorist. The man was battered and bleeding from several cuts around the face. But the fact that he was alive meant he'd fared far better than any of his comrades. His eyes were wide. He'd heard the three shots from the Beretta, and his gaze locked on the bleeding body of his commander and leader, Eid Farid.

Now, to his utter terror, the very same gun was directed at his own heart. And the American said, almost in a whisper, "I want to know where the second attack is taking place and I want to know now."

The terrorist told him.

FIFTEEN MINUTES LATER Salah Abi's squad car halted at Deir Amba Samaan, the Monastery of St. Simeon. The stone, turreted walls rose eighteen feet, and behind them was the monastery, carved out of a steep hill.

The guard at the front gate was about to ask them for an admission charge when he spotted the ID Abi waved at him and the guns both the men had drawn. He paled.

They stepped quickly across the open courtyard. The buildings, dating from the sixth and seventh centuries, were built like a medieval fortress with heavy stone walls. The structures that served as the home to the long-gone Christian order were as solid as any pyramid erected four thousand years earlier. They were impressive, but still near the end of most sight-seeing lists. Bolan scanned the openings to the various rooms and displays, seeing no one. No signs of terrorist activity. No sign of anything.

Another guard strolled casually around the corner and

stopped cold when he spotted the two gunmen, until Abi waved his identification and gestured for silence.

"Police," he whispered.

"What's going on?" the guard asked worriedly.

"I need to know how many people are inside the monastery."

The guard was confused. "I don't know for sure. Two or three groups of sightseers, maybe. And the university group."

"University group?"

"Christian studies group from a university in America. They wanted to see the bedrooms in the upper levels. There is nothing up there but bats now, but they got official permission."

"How many in the group?" Bolan asked.

"I am not sure. Thirty. Thirty-five."

"That's the target," Bolan stated. "Where's the way up?"

The guard pointed to a set of stairs across the courtyard, leading up the steep hillside into the monastery. A family emerged from one of the ground-level doorways, the father looking at a brochure, two kids looking bored.

"Get those people out of here quickly and quietly," Abi ordered the guard. "Alert the others up front where we've gone."

Bolan was already racing toward the stairs, irregularly spaced stone steps that showed the wear of fourteen centuries. He bounded up them, the Heckler & Koch MP-5 A-3 up and ready. Abi followed but fell behind quickly.

It didn't take any warrior's senses to detect the sudden blast of automatic-rifle fire that erupted above him and the screams that followed moments later. Bolan detected as many as five weapons firing in the chaotic noise, five automatic weapons trained on a crowd of unsuspecting, unarmed civilians in an enclosed space....

He didn't need to call up a mental picture of the possibilities because within seconds he reached the top of the stairs, and the slaughter lay before him. There were five gunmen, Arabs in robes, with scarves covering the lower halves of their faces. They were strategically scattered around a wide main area that might have once served as a dining room or social area. Two were to Bolan's left. Three more were firing from the other side of the room, one near to a thick stone column, the others in the doorway of the next room. It wasn't difficult to imagine how they had stepped out of their hiding places just moments ago.

The guard had underestimated the number in the university group. Bolan knew there were at least forty people here. As many as ten were already dead. The rest were screaming and running in every direction or curling on the floor in helpless fetal balls. One brave but foolish man was running directly at one of the assassins as if to wrestle the assault rifle from his grasp, and was being stitched across the chest with 7.62 mm rounds.

Bolan saw all this and recorded the details in the blink of an eye. In less time than that he had evaluated his own strategy and begun acting on it. He leveled the Heckler & Koch at the man next to the pillar, whose Kalashnikov was doing the most damage, and let loose with a burst that blasted the gunner backward onto the stone floor.

The Executioner spun quickly, confronting the two gunners on the other side of the room. He was wide open to them, since they didn't care about firing through the mass of innocent people. He didn't have that luxury; he shot above their heads, ripping chunks of rock from the wall around them and the ceiling above them. They retreated through the door and behind the walls.

Bolan sank behind the low railing just in time to avoid the blast of the nearest terrorist. He let eight rounds singe the air above him, then instinctively felt a pause. Propelling himself to his feet, he leaned on the trigger. The 9 mm parabellum rounds blasted at the spot where the nearest gunner had been, but he had ducked out of sight. Bolan redirected the stream of bullets at the second gunner, who was still in the process of jumping for cover. The blast ripped at his arm, and the man was wrenched into the open, where more rounds ate into his chest and throat. Both he and his gun dropped to the stone floor.

The Executioner checked for the gunners on the far side of the room, ignoring the screams and sobbing of the civilians. There was no trace of them, but he fired at the doorway again, reminding them of his presence. He knew the Heckler & Koch was almost empty, and as the clip ran dry he was already extracting the Desert Eagle from the holster on his hip.

"He's out of ammo—get him now!" It was the nearest of the terrorists, unaware that his companions were dead or had fled. He jumped to his feet, leveling the assault rifle. Bolan was already triggering the Desert Eagle, and the first .44-caliber round cratered into the Arab's chest, which exploded with flesh and blood.

Salah Abi had reached the top of the stairs, shouting into his radio for emergency medical personnel, who were already en route to the monastery.

"Two more went through there," Bolan said, nodding at the doorway beyond the mass of dead and wounded. He reholstered the Desert Eagle and slammed another magazine into the MP-5 A-3, then threaded his way among the mayhem, flattening again the stone wall on the far side of the room. He glanced through the doorway and saw no one. Stepping through, he maintained the subgun at gut level, ready to fire.

He faced a series of open archways, a few retaining the iron hinges that had once held wooden doors, long since rotted away. The gunmen were hiding in one of them.

Bolan waited just seconds as his eyes adjusted to the dim light. He could still hear the cries of the wounded and terrified civilians, and above it he made out a strange rustling noise. Bats. He stepped forward silently in the shadows and listened more closely. The bats that lived in the old monks' bedrooms, disturbed by the intruders, were fluttering and shifting. In another ten seconds he had pinpointed which one of the rooms contained the disturbed animals.

Bolan unclipped a CS smoke grenade from the military webbing under his shirt. With the flick of a finger, he activated the canister and tossed it into the black room. The plumes of smoke ejected from the door with a muffled burst, the billows filling the room and panicking the occupants.

The flutter turned to a rush of wings and high-pitched squeals of confusion and fear as several thousand Egyptian fruit bats took to the air at once and burst out of the room in a steady torrent. Bolan ignored them, knowing they would avoid him by echolocation despite their terror at being driven from their dark hole into foreign daylight. With the sound came the screams of the gunmen, who rushed out of the room, waving their arms frantically above their heads and faces. They raised their guns as if in vain hopes of clearing a safe escape path. Bolan triggered the subgun, and the blind, frantic gunmen danced at the end of the stream of 9 mm parabellum rounds before dropping to the stone floor.

6

The cost for a private room on the train from Aswân to Luxor was exorbitant, but Bolan had appropriated several thousand dollars from the drug runners working for Satish Malkani in Saudi Arabia and didn't have second thoughts about using it to buy himself a decent night's rest.

After his eradication of the attack force at Deir Amba Samaan, the cleanup had been extensive. Fourteen of forty-two innocent U.S. travelers were in the morgue, and another seventeen were in the hospital. A room-by-room search of the monastery had turned up no more members of the Holy Voice, just a few tourists hiding from the gunfire.

Back at Salah Abi's office, they had laid out the pieces of the puzzle as they knew them, and those pieces were few in number. The location of the phone that had issued the target commands turned out to be a public phone on a street in Luxor, another tourist city in the middle of the country, brimming with spectacular archaeological attractions. Luxor was built literally on top of the ancient city of Thebes, and many ancient monuments were still in existence. Nearby was the West Bank, with its neighborhood of ancient temples and the Valley of the Kings, perhaps the most famous burying place on earth.

The city offered even more potential for terror by the Holy Voice than did Aswân. But when Bolan awakened after seven solid hours of rest, he was ready to take on whatever the Holy Voice's Luxor cell had to throw at him.

By 8:00 a.m. he was stepping from the train. Taking it had allowed him to reach the town several hours ahead of any of the flights available out of Aswân that morning. He had an entire day ahead of him.

His first stop was a pay phone in the train station, where he accessed a secure line such as the GDSSI could provide. Salah Abi got on the line, sounding weary. Bolan had agreed to work with the agency, though he'd made it clear he would be acting on his own, at his own discretion, and using whatever means he saw fit.

"Mr. Belasko, I hope you slept better than I."

"Anything new?"

"No, my friend. We have put all our questions to the widows of the Holy Voice you made yesterday. They were mostly hysterical, of course. They knew nothing at all."

"It was worth a try. What about the search of their building. Any clues?"

"No help there. But I do have one interesting tidbit for you. A contact within the agency who already has a lead into the Luxor camp of the Holy Voice."

"Why haven't we heard of him until now?"

"Because his mission is highly classified. Very few within the agency even know about him, and fewer still knew that the group he was infiltrating was the Holy Voice. The agency watches many different groups. In fact, I might never have heard about him without Mr. Brognola's influence. Just what does Mr. Brognola have on my boss?"

"You've got me. But I'm glad he does. Give me the details."

"Abdul Assad. He spent eighteen years in the Egyptian army, the last four in intelligence. He was recruited by our agency's antiterrorist department when it was formed just a year ago. He's been on the streets of Luxor ever since, trying to get tight with a local group called Unsullied Islam, suspected of a few murders over the past couple of years and which has only in the past several months come under Kazem Emad's wing. The members of the groups were inspired by Emad's vision, and the convenient disappearance of their own founder, who did *not* see eye to eye with Emad, helped speed the bonding process. Anyway, we have an in."

"That's good news. When can I meet this Assad?"

"This morning. The bad news is that he is convinced we're on the wrong track. He says the group in Luxor is not an important body within the Holy Voice, and he is sure Emad is not in the city. He suggests we keep looking in Aswân."

Bolan considered that. "I don't agree. I believe Emad's trying to keep himself at arm's length during what he considers to be just preliminary moves, and that means he'll stay outside the strike zones. I have a feeling Aswân has been used up. I'll meet with Assad and see what he has to offer in terms of hard Intel."

Abi rattled off a street address. "He's there this morning. You can get there in twenty minutes by taxi."

"It's his house? Is it safe for his cover if I show up there?"

"His cover is that he's an international investor—whatever that means—and he has an office in his home. He has Americans and Europeans coming and going daily."

The taxi driver nodded at the address and had him there well within the predicted twenty minutes. Bolan found himself in front of a modest home. A Mercedes was parked in the driveway, but was ten years old and had lost its luster. The inside of the home, too, looked less than opulent when a young man silently ushered Bolan inside.

"It is now prayer time," the boy said in stiff English. "Mr. Assad will be with you in a short while."

Bolan nodded and sat in a small office, beside a desk cluttered with import-tax forms. He glanced over them briefly and found that Mr. Assad's investments seemed to be in used manufacturing equipment, which he was bringing in at rock-bottom prices.

"It is to stimulate manufacturing within Egypt and to cause Egypt to thrive—a noble cause, in the eyes of Unsullied Islam." Abdul Assad stepped into the room and took Bolan's hand in a firm, strong shake. He was a tall, lanky man, with a mass of very thick, dark hair streaked with gray. His dark eyes appraised Bolan frankly. "We may talk here. The office is bugged, but it is bugged by the agency, not the Holy Voice. I am Abdul Assad."

Bolan introduced himself, using the Michael Belasko alias.

"Salah Abi told me you were almost single-handedly responsible for foiling the attempts of the Holy Voice to murder more tourists yesterday."

"I didn't do so well. Fourteen innocent people died."

Assad nodded. "Fourteen instead of forty-two was the report I was given. Or far more than forty-two if the museum attack had succeeded, as well. You tracked down the Holy Voice, helped head off their attack at the Aswân Archaeological Museum and effectively wiped out the St. Simeon attack force. That's not Abi's exaggerated conversation, either. That's his official report, which leaves me wondering what kind of American the agency has recruited."

"I'm not officially working for the agency."

"CIA?" Assad was a man who refused to take a hint.

"Independent," Bolan stated. "Tell me how closely you're involved with the Holy Voice and what you've learned from them."

Assad leaned back and made a gesture with his hands that was the equivalent of a shrug. "Very well. Several times I met some low-level lieutenants of the Luxor group, which was then calling itself Unsullied Islam, and become quite friendly with them. It is easy to make the rounds once you make your political views clear. Egypt contains some very distinct ideological segmentation. I am sure you know about the Brotherhood. The Brotherhood has been in existence since the twenties and is getting very old and stodgy in the views of many Egyptians. It has become a political party. Worse, it has become a bureaucracy. It accomplishes nothing in the eyes of many Egyptians, who want their nation to become a true Islamic state.

"The Brotherhood has always had its extremist members. They've been becoming less popular with the peace-loving majority of members. Especially in the last couple of years and especially since last year's summit of Islamic nations in Casablanca. You are familiar with this? The assembled heads of the Islamic nations agreed to a campaign against extremism and Muslim violence. That's when the agency was formed."

Bolan nodded. "Yes. This was the catalyst for extremists within the Brotherhood to leave the group?"

"Exactly. And of course, once they left the Brotherhood they started their own small, single-purpose organizations, and no longer were buffered by mitigating points of view from less violently inclined Egyptians. They went untempered. Their rationale was less often challenged. And so it increasingly sounds sensible within their close-knit memberships. That's when the groups like Unsullied Islam started really picking up speed."

Bolan wasn't unfamiliar with the phenomenon. "So you acted sympathetic to what you knew to be the points of view of Unsullied Islam and were able to find its members here in Luxor?"

"Exactly. It wasn't difficult. And it wasn't difficult to engage them in conversation, at cafés and other social places. Getting into their meetings has proved more difficult, especially since they have been absorbed into the group known as the Holy Voice. They no longer even use the name Unsullied Islam day to day. I'm only now starting to establish a level of trust between myself and some of the top-level captains of the Luxor branch."

"Does your cover make you more suspicious in their eyes?"

"It did at first, certainly. But then they understood my motivation—to bring technology and industry into Egypt, to make it a more independent nation, to make it a strong individual among the Muslim states. They don't argue the advantages of industrialism if industry is operated by Muslims under precepts of *sharia*, Islamic law, in the ways that it applies."

"So who leads the Luxor group? And how tight are you with him?"

"Manal Faragall. Not tight, but getting there."

"And Kazem Emad?"

"He's visited the group twice that I know of, and he was present when I visited the homes of one of their members. I was formally introduced to him and was pretty carefully given the once-over. I seemed to pass muster.

"My impression was that he was in town on a visit at that time. He was staying with Faragall. Emad is certainly not based here in Luxor. But I did overhear references made by him to Aswân, fairly strong references that convinced me he's based there. That's what I told Abi."

"So he said. I find that hard to believe. His biography shows no ties to Aswân, and surely it's not the single best staging ground in Egypt for what he has in mind. Abi's reports of his early activities indicated there are small groups tied to the Holy Voice in several Egyptian cities.

That's why I've come looking for him here. Luxor may be where he decides to strike next."

Assad made the shrugging gesture again with his hands. "Believe what you like. I certainly hope Abi maintains his search of Aswân, however. I'm sure that's where the break-throughs are going to come in this investigation."

"Have you heard anything about attacks planned on tourists or foreigners?"

"My impression is that the group might be leading up to something. But I'm not in *that* tight. If they've got something in the works in the near future they haven't involved me."

"What about Nabil Aman?"

There was a flicker in Assad's eyes, noticeable but un-readable. "I know nothing about him. I've never met him or heard his name mentioned among Unsullied Islam. I've certainly not had any indication of a master strategist train-ing Luxor members for the kind of attacks you're expecting."

Bolan considered that, and considered Abdul Assad. The man was sophisticated, educated and as blank as a wall, revealing nothing. Maybe it was just a trait he'd acquired in his line of work. Maybe more. Perhaps he resented the fact that his cover was suddenly being exploited by this American, who showed up out of nowhere and wasn't even a part of the agency or GDSSI. Perhaps he was worried that his cover, to which he had, after all, devoted a year of his life, might be compromised. Bolan wasn't going to make any assumptions yet.

"We believe that the Holy Voice will be acting again soon. Maybe here, maybe elsewhere. I'd like you to apply a little pressure, make them think you're getting anxious to belong. See what they tell you."

Assad considered that and nodded slightly. "What is your intent in the meantime?"

"Watch them. See if I can learn anything as an outside observer. Can you tell me where they meet?"

The nod this time was even more reluctant. "I can give you the addresses of the three homes I've been to. There is no central meeting place. They meet in different homes and cafés and move often, specifically to avoid all getting caught together or traced too easily."

"Fine. I'll start with those three sites."

Assad leaned forward and quickly jotted down three addresses.

"You'll have to be extremely careful. None of these neighborhoods are used to American visitors."

Bolan took the sheet. "I'm good at blending in."

"I wrote the name of a hotel, as well. It's a small place, frequented by foreigners who come to this city often, like businessmen. It's not touristy and it's not someplace where you'll be seen by a lot of people."

Bolan nodded. "Call me there when you know anything."

The young houseman appeared when Assad touched a button on his desk and Bolan was ushered out. He wondered if the Egyptian agent really felt such staged formality necessary. He had other doubts about Abdul Assad, inexplicable doubts fired only by a warrior's instinct.

As he stepped into the vestibule behind the houseman, a side door opened. A woman, fully wrapped in robes and scarves, appeared quickly and looked frankly at Bolan for a moment. He could see nothing but her forehead and eyes, but those eyes were red and strained, not so much from recent sobbing as with long-lived fear.

She closed the door again, just as quickly.

He left with the feeling that Abdul Assad hadn't given him a complete picture of the situation in Luxor. Perhaps the agent was suspicious of Bolan. He was an American and a non-Muslim, involved, through no choice of Assad's, in what was an Egyptian and an Islamic problem. Maybe the man was feeling manipulated, as if his work and authority were being undermined.

If so, the Executioner hoped he would get his head together and deal with the situation as it now was. Bolan didn't have the time or inclination to contend with bruised egos and stepped-on toes.

FOURTEEN HOURS LATER he was in no better spirits.

After spending the day staking out the addresses supplied by Assad, he had come up empty-handed, having seen nothing more sinister than a group of old women cooking a meal and a handful of children being put to bed. He managed to sneak unseen into two of the houses and search the meager rooms, finding nothing that connected them in any way to the Holy Voice. There had been no male visitors to any of the homes that might indicate a meeting or exchange of views or information. When two brothers, men of their house, went out for a while in the evening they walked a few steps to a decrepit café, where they had sugared tea and told outlandish jokes in Arabic. They did nothing that even looked suspicious, then went home to their families and slept.

Bolan decided to do the same and approach Assad again in the morning for better intelligence.

He found the hotel Assad recommended and took a room on the third floor. It was a humble, clean building with a fair enough view of the surrounding city and an attractive courtyard, which Bolan's room overlooked. The soldier pulled the thin curtain and spent twenty minutes organizing his backpack and preparing for bed. Then he lay down and turned out the light.

In the darkness Bolan crawled out of bed to the floor and crept across the room on his hands and knees, sure that no one who might be looking in from outside would see his moving silhouette. He stepped into the tiny closet and pulled the rickety slatted door shut, the Beretta 93-R in a state of readiness in his grip.

He'd been thinking about his meeting with the quietly pretentious Abdul Assad, and the more he considered him, the more the soldier was convinced the man was playing a game of deception. At best. Bolan's day of fruitless watching seemed to bear this out. Those addresses hadn't been genuine leads to members of the Luxor cell, just harmless Egyptian families.

Maybe Assad was simply stupid, and was being played as a pawn by Unsullied Islam. Maybe all the leads he'd reported to the agency up to this point had been false leads supplied by the terrorists. Maybe his office was bugged, unbeknownst to Assad, by the terrorists, and they had been warned of Bolan stakeouts and had warned the residents of those homes to act normally. None of the possibilities was flattering to Assad. But some painted him as a fool and some painted him as a murderous traitor. Bolan was still feeling generous enough to give the man the benefit of the doubt.

He started feeling differently when he heard the first noise just outside his room.

Late at night there was a little traffic to mask the cautious footsteps, but Bolan heard them clearly through the slats in the closet door. A figure approached, stopped at the soldier's room and inserted, one tooth at a time, a key into the flimsy doorknob. The knob was turned slowly to release the lock with only a muffled thump.

At the same moment there was a rustle outside the window, and a head appeared behind the blind, lifted the curtain back onto its hook and looked around the room. The covers on the bed had been left arranged in the darkness so that a figure might very well have been lying there sleeping. The intruder never even glanced at the closet.

The man in the window stepped inside with a long, gleaming blade. Another figure appeared behind him and guarded the window. They had to have been standing on a ladder. The man in the hall also waited in his place. He was sent simply to guard the exit and render assistance if needed. No chances were being taken.

Bolan watched the man in the window, whose head was turned toward the bed, without thought for any of the other shadows in the room. The Executioner eased out of the closet.

The would-be assassin raised the massive blade above his head as if about to deliver a ceremonial decapitation, then grunted in surprise and whipped back the blankets.

At that moment Bolan fired the Beretta, and the guard outside the window never knew he was dead. He simply dropped from sight. The sound of the three suppressed rounds was audible enough for the attacker to hear. He whirled, but by then the soldier had aimed the handgun in his direction. The Beretta coughed three more rounds, and the knife wielder toppled onto the bed with a series of bounces. Bolan aimed at the door and fired off a burst, the rounds punching through the thin panels of wood. He opened the door quickly and grabbed the mass of material his hand came in contact with, dragging it into the room. The man was dying and loosening his grip on an automatic in his left hand. It dropped to the bare floor with a loud thud. The gunman was glaring at Bolan with abject hatred, which remained on his face when his final breath rattled out.

Bolan checked the man on the bed and found him also dead, then stepped to the window. There was indeed a wooden ladder propped against the side of the building. All he could see of the window guard was a pair of feet protruding from the shadows around a low growth of shrubbery against the building.

The soldier retrieved his backpack from the closet and locked the door again, then exited the room via the ladder. He hid the ladder with its dead owner in the shadows, where it was unlikely they would be discovered before first light.

The day hadn't been productive, but Bolan had a feeling his first night in Luxor would be.

7

"This is Belasko."

The end of the line was quiet, then Abdul Assad said levelly, "Why are you contacting me at this time of the night?"

"The Holy Voice knows I'm in town. I was attacked at the hotel."

"You must have been careless this afternoon. I warned you about the dangers of a white man sneaking around an Arab neighborhood. You escaped, I take it."

"I survived."

"And your attackers?"

"They didn't."

Bolan could hear the Egyptian agent breathing on the other end of the line but couldn't tell how this news affected him.

"Congratulations. How many were there?"

"Three. I left them at the hotel. The maid is in for a shock. I won't be going back there, of course. We need to talk."

"Now?"

"Yes. I managed to get Intel from one of them before he expired," Bolan lied. "Information I know you'll find interesting."

"Really?"

If Bolan's instincts were on target, he'd just planted some potent seeds of doubt in Assad's mind.

"All right. Come to—"

"I'll meet you at a place called Mall of Osiris. Know it?"

"Yes. A tourist place near the hotel strip. I thought you were going to avoid tourist spots."

"Yeah, and look how much good it did me. I'll be there in about one hour. I've got another stop to make first."

"All right, Mr. Belasko. I will meet you there."

Bolan hung up. He was, in fact, standing in the parking lot just outside the Mall of Osiris, a two-story structure much like any mall in the U.S. except for the fact that it was largely open to the mild Egyptian climate.

Heading inside, he found the place consisted of a couple of dozen shops, none larger than a small drugstore and some no more than tiny stalls. The roof was just a framework intended to shade the retail areas; in a city that experienced less than an inch of precipitation a year, that was all that was needed. In the middle was a courtyard area with a now-silent fountain and border of stubby palm trees and low green growth planted in boxes. The wrought-iron chairs were turned up on the tables in the café area, and the three food booths were enclosed by security hoods. The shops, as well, were shuttered or covered with steel gates. The mall was in darkness except for a few antiburglar floodlights, spaced too far apart to be truly effective.

Bolan began his recon of the place. If he had guessed correctly, he would be joined by Assad, or whomever the man sent, in much less than an hour. And instead of lying in wait for Bolan, the Executioner would be lying in wait for them.

One of the smaller stalls was covered in front with a gate that slotted into grooves in the floor and ceiling. A section of the gate opened like a door. Bolan contemplated its position compared to the courtyard, strategy automatically beginning to form in his warrior's brain.

There was no alarm system tied to the gate. He withdrew his picks and had the padlock on the steel gate open in less than a minute. Inside he found the usual tourist merchandise. There were glass shelves loaded with plastic replicas of the archaeological attractions: a sphinx, a step pyramid and the multiple-columned temple of Luxor. A wall-mounted set of swinging bars was draped with low-quality rugs. Bolan shifted the bars of the display so that several of the rugs were swung to the front of the stall. A man could stand within those rugs and be unseen. The stall owner wouldn't have approved. In this position the rugs could have been reached with an outstretched hand through the bars of the gate.

But Bolan wasn't interested in stealing rugs.

Closing the gate behind him, he crossed the courtyard to the stores on the opposite end of the mall. Here the common area turned a corner and was hidden from the central courtyard. Near the south entrance he found a glass-fronted shop that appeared to be a step above the others, at least in terms of the price of its merchandise. He made quick work of the lock in the glass door and let himself inside, making directly for the display window, which held a mummy case. The case was wooden and deep, and its occupant was nothing more than a life-size rag doll wrapped in linen. Bolan removed the fake mummy and hid it behind the store counter. The empty case was so shadowed in the dim light that it was impossible to tell whether there was anything inside it.

Bolan departed the store, again leaving it unlocked, and heard the sound of approaching cars. Less than fifteen minutes had passed since the soldier hung up the phone. Assad was working fast. The Executioner found a hiding place behind a tree on the far side of the courtyard. He could hear the opening and closing of several car doors and the approaching footsteps of what had to have been ten or so men. The group headed directly to the courtyard, gathering just a few yards from the hidden warrior, and one of them began to issue orders.

"We're going to spread out, get into hiding and be ready to spring on the bastard the moment he reaches this spot. Samir, take two men and hide behind the back of the mall outside the south entrance. Attia, hide two men behind the back of the north entrance. Listen for my signal. I'll radio for you to spring the trap. At that time I want you to move into position across the entrances. Be ready to gun him down when he tries to run. Hopefully he won't get that far."

Bolan had been certain immediately that the man in charge wasn't Assad. He listened now to the monosyllabic responses for any voice that might belong to the agency contact. But Assad, even if he was a part of the Holy Voice, wouldn't necessarily be one of their guns. He might have simply called in a report and allowed the hardmen in the outfit to set the snare.

The Luxor captain began to shout orders. "Ahmed, find the light box. When I give the signal, I want this place full of lights. I want it bright as day. I don't want any mistakes made. I don't want us shooting at each other in the dark. Eliwa, Vasif and myself will find hiding places here in the courtyard. Abdul, you sit right there. Whatever you do, stay here. Make him come to you. Don't let him draw you outside the mall. As long as he's within these walls, he's ours."

"Certainly."

That was Assad, and any lingering doubts Bolan might have had about the man's betrayal melted. His presence meant he was fair game as far as the Executioner was concerned.

He'd counted eleven men total: three at each end, four,

including Assad, in the middle, and the man assigned to work the lights. Bolan began to fine-tune his strategies.

He didn't have long. One of the hardmen had decided the large tree would make a decent hiding place and was heading in his direction.

"And remember," the group leader said to the scattering men, "to keep silent until the trap is sprung."

The approaching hardman nodded. Bolan quickly placed all the other members as they sought cover. He'd have to take out the man quietly, and no matter what, there would be a dangerous risk of being heard. Even the slightest sound might alert Assad, who was removing the chairs from one of the small wrought-iron tables and sitting, or the captain and the other hardmen who had been assigned to find stakeout spots in the courtyard area.

The hardman walked around the far side of the tree without looking where he was going. Bolan looped his length of nylon cord around the man's neck, and the slip-knot tightened instantly, stifling the tiny gasp of alarm that escaped the man's lips. He tried to recoil from the sudden sensation of suffocation, swinging his autorifle at Bolan, who grabbed it and used it to lever the man to the ground on his back. The soldier slammed his victim's chin with the butt of his palm, causing the man's head to twist sideways too fast and too hard for his spine to withstand the pressure. There was a simple pop from his neck, and suddenly he was limp. Bolan released the end of the cord and let it slip free from the corpse's neck.

He relieved the dead man of his radio, which was set to receive but was silent, waiting for the call to attack. Bolan turned it off.

One terrorist down and ten to go.

He waited in the darkness for five minutes. Predictably one of the nearby men started to get weary of standing in the same position and started to shift; in that moment Bolan spotted him. He was sitting on the ground behind the low brick wall that surrounded the fountain. His dark silhouette was mirrored by the silent water when he moved, though when he was still even the Executioner had trouble making him out in the darkness.

The soldier sank to the floor and began to creep around the back of the courtyard area, against the outer wall. He came to the edge of the fountain and followed the low wall until he was within a couple yards of his intended victim. The man was getting uncomfortable again. He shifted into a cross-legged position and carelessly allowed his autorifle to scrape the stone wall. Untrained, he was a killer, nonetheless. Bolan felt no pity for him and made his move while the man was getting a better sitting position.

The first awareness the man had of Bolan was of an iron hand clamping over his mouth. His second awareness was the bright, piercing sensation that came as the Ka-bar fighting knife cut through the flesh of his throat, severing his jugular and slicing through his windpipe.

Then he had no more awareness whatsoever.

Bolan propped the corpse in position behind the wall so that, in the darkness at least, he appeared to be patiently waiting for the call to attack.

The final courtyard hardman, the one who had been barking the orders, was hidden behind the second of the three food booths, across several yards of open, cobbled courtyard. Assad was the only other man in sight. He couldn't reach either of them without risking being seen. Bolan had reached an impasse.

Suddenly the leader's radio squawked and Bolan saw Assad almost leap to his feet in alarm.

The commander brought his radio to his mouth quickly. "Faragall."

"Ahmed here. I can't find a set of circuit breakers. It

looks like they've got a single switch for all the primary lighting."

The captain stood up behind his cart and faced to the north, in the direction the speaker was coming from.

"What's the matter?" Assad hissed.

Bolan knew he wouldn't have a better chance. He risked it, bolting from behind the low fountain wall and across what seemed an interminable stretch of open darkness. If there had been more than the faintest light, either of the men would have glimpsed him peripherally. He flattened against the wall and edged along its surface as the conversation between the captain and the light operator wound down. He crept flat along the storefronts until he turned the corner and was out of their line of sight.

The south entrance to the mall was wide open and empty. Bolan headed toward it and stopped several paces from the ungated entrance. Somewhere outside were three gunman, waiting for him. He turned on his radio at very low volume.

The captain was muttering orders gruffly over the tiny speaker. Bolan determined he was telling the radio operator to be ready to throw the lights on command. He listened closely to the captain's tone and accent, and after a few more quiet minutes he activated the "send" on his stolen radio and did a passable job imitating him.

"Lights!" he commanded.

Somewhere in a mall security office, the operator jumped to the control and activated it. The overhead lights blazed on, illuminating the retail center as if it were opening for business. Bolan heard cries in both directions. The south-entrance guards took the sudden call for lights as the signal, assuming their intended victim had come in at the opposite end of the mall, and they ran inside at full speed, ready to render assistance.

Bolan had already leveled the MP-5 A-3 and triggered

it as the three Arabs appeared in the open. The autofire ripped into them one after another, stopping them in their tracks and throwing them into a jerky dance of death.

Three more down. Cries of confusion rang out from behind him.

Yanking open the glass door, Bolan slipped into the souvenir shop, shutting off his radio. The store's lights were individually controlled, and the shop remained dark.

The soldier knew he had scant seconds to get to cover. If one or both of the dead guards in the courtyard had been spotted, he might have a few seconds more. He stepped onto the display-window ledge and nestled himself backward into the mummy case.

He wasn't as well hidden as he had anticipated he would be. The mall lights were bright enough they reached in and dimly illuminated the lower half of his body. He wouldn't stand up to close scrutiny. But he didn't intend to permit anyone the time to closely scrutinize him.

A single man appeared, running, with a radio in his left hand and a Soviet-made AK-74 in the other. He slowed to a stop when he spotted the corpses, registering disbelief on his gaunt face.

"He got them! All three!"

The gunman's voice identified him as the captain of the attack force. "I don't know where he went, though. I didn't pass him. Attia, get into the parking lot. He may be making a break for it. Shoot him on sight! Assad, do you see anything?"

"Nothing. Are you sure he's not hiding somewhere?"

The captain suddenly realized his mistake and jumped like a startled cat. "Ahmed, get those lights off! Get them off right now!"

It was too late for the captain. He had wandered almost directly in front of the warrior.

Maybe a sense of his impending doom alerted the terrorist leader. Something made him crane his neck suddenly to his right. He saw what appeared to be a mummy in the store window. It had come to life and was aiming a Heckler & Koch MP-5 A-3 at him.

Bolan triggered the weapon just as the lights died throughout the mall. His view was distorted as the bullets crashed through the window and the glass shattered into thousands of pebble-sized pieces. The captain was flung to the floor as the 9 mm rounds cut across his abdomen and wrist. His AK-74 clattered on the cobblestones.

That was six down. Five to go.

Bolan stepped from the ruin of the window and made his way back to the courtyard, close to the wall and ready to leap for cover should the lights be restored.

There was no sign of life. Assad might have fled, or he might be hiding, as well. There were several good places in the darkened courtyard. The Executioner judged that Assad wasn't the type to stick around in a dangerous situation, but he wasn't about to risk his life on that assessment by blundering into the open. He waited.

But not for long. He heard the brush of feet on the stone far ahead and made out the shifting of shadows. Three men approached in a staggered formation. Bolan guessed they were the guards from the north entrance. They waited outside the courtyard opposite Bolan and tried to make out the scene in the darkness. They couldn't. The soldier heard one get on the radio and alert the light operator to turn on the lights.

A moment later the lights blazed on, and Bolan stepped out from the wall, triggering a blistering figure eight at the three guards. The man with the radio was saved by lightning reflexes and dived to his left, behind one of the food booths, screaming in pain as two 9 mm rounds mangled his leg. The other two men had time only to cry out and attempt some action with their own autorifles. The 9 mm rounds shook their bodies until they collapsed. The subgun clicked dry, and Bolan dropped it.

The wounded man knew the sound and crawled out from behind the food booth, bringing his own Kalashnikov into play. He hadn't counted on the Executioner instantly withdrawing the Desert Eagle. The .44 Magnum blast hit the downed terrorist like a small truck, knocking him on his back, sending his weapon flying and shattering his sternum and collarbone.

And then there were two: the light operator and, somewhere, the traitorous Abdul Assad.

A small metallic creak came from the north end. Bolan bolted forward, but the north entrance was empty when he reached it. He stepped outside briefly. No one was in the lot. Assad was inside, somewhere, hiding.

Bolan flipped on his stolen radio and instantly heard, "Hello! Somebody give me a report!"

"Lights off!" Bolan ordered.

"Faragall? Is that you?"

"Lights off!"

No more protests or questions were forthcoming, and a few seconds later the lights throughout the mall were gone.

Waiting inside the north entrance, Bolan listened hard in the silence. There was a movement in one of the storefronts. Bolan was almost amused to realize it was in the other souvenir store he had unlocked. Assad had to have been trying every gate he passed in his flight, in a desperate attempt for a hiding place. And the movement Bolan had seen was a slight shift among the hanging rugs, which made the small metallic creak.

Quickly he crossed the mall walkway and approached the storefront, and from that angle Assad couldn't see what he was up to. He peered around the wall to rest the muzzle of the Desert Eagle between the metal sections of the gate. He fired into the midst of the rugs, blasting holes through several of them. And through to Abdul Assad. He fell to the floor of the shop, wailing, clutching at a shallow but wideopen spot in his left pectoral.

Bolan nudged the gate with his foot, and it squeaked open. He stood over the traitor.

Assad's eyes rolled up at the Executioner, and from somewhere he produced a small-caliber pistol. The Desert Eagle spoke again like thunder, and the traitor's gun was flung away, his hand transformed into a mass of raw flesh. He began to scream anew.

In the ruckus Bolan almost missed the approaching footsteps. The light operator, Ahmed, had finally realized the situation had gone seriously wrong.

Bolan reached around the corner, intending to fire on the newcomer when he stepped into view, then heard the runner come to a halt just before stepping into the open—obviously contemplating the corpses of the north-entrance guards.

The end food booth served as Ahmed's cover. He crouched behind it and leveled his assault rifle at the end of the mall, looking for the source of the screaming, confident the enemy was in that vicinity.

Assad's vision cleared enough to witness Bolan peering around the corner.

"Here!" he yelled in warning. "He's in here!"

The gunman fired blindly in the direction of the store. The 7.62 mm rounds bounced off the cobblestones and rattled the gate.

Bolan didn't respond, hoping the gunman would assume he'd hit him and come looking.

But nothing came out of the darkness. The waiting game was getting old. Bolan aimed for the edge of the booth at approximately the spot he knew the gunman should be. He fired, and the .44 Magnum round gouged an inch of wood off the corner of the booth hood. There was a cry of alarm and the sound of footsteps running away.

Bolan raced from the store. By the time he'd reached the courtyard, the footsteps had disappeared around the corner in the direction of the south entrance. When the Executioner rounded the corner, he saw the running figure hurdling the body of the dead captain. Bolan fired on the run, fell into a crouch and fired again. He couldn't tell where he'd struck the runner, but Ahmed tumbled to the floor, using his momentum to roll onto his back. He shouted and raised the Soviet assault rifle, firing in Bolan's general direction. The shots dug into the ceiling.

A well-placed shot from the Desert Eagle ended the terrorist's pain. Bolan approached the man and kicked the gun away, checking the man's condition. A low rumble reached him—a car engine starting.

He sprinted through the south entrance and around the end of the building, spotting a Mercedes tearing from the parking lot, a single figure visible inside. It bounced over a curb, still gaining speed, swung wildly into the street and accelerated into the night.

It could only have been Abdul Assad.

8

When he emerged from the ruin and slaughter in the Mall of Osiris, Bolan found a figure in long robes waiting for him in the parking lot, directly under a streetlight. The retrieved and reloaded MP-5 A-3 was instantly leveled at the newcomer, who gazed at it impassively. Bolan approached the figure steadily, waiting for any sudden movement that would motivate him to trigger the weapon. The movement didn't come.

"I'm Ara."

That told him nothing. The Executioner waited for more.

"I saw Abdul drive off. Is he the only one left?"

Bolan came to within two yards of the woman before stopping.

"You're the woman I saw in Assad's house yesterday morning."

"Yes."

"What are you doing here?"

"I've come to help you. And to escape Abdul Assad and Kazem Emad."

"What's your connection to them?"

"Surely there are emergency vehicles on the way here by now. Shouldn't we leave?"

"Take off that robe."

"Mr. Belasko, I am a Muslim and a woman!"

"I don't care if you're the pope. Remove the robe—slowly."

Ara deliberately unwrapped the robe, letting it fall to the pavement. Underneath she wore heavy slacks, a full linen shirt and a beige vest. She combed her fingers through her hair, and the headpiece dropped away, revealing long hair. She had been transformed into a woman who wouldn't look out of place on any street in the Western world.

She raised her arms to her sides, as if to prove she was unarmed.

Distantly they heard the whooping of an emergency-vehicle siren.

"All right," Bolan said, "let's go."

They marched into the darkness, and Bolan retrieved his backpack, which he had stashed behind a shrub prior to staking out the mall. Minutes later they found themselves in a dark, deserted area of middle-class homes.

"Where are we headed?"

"You tell me. Where will Assad go?"

"Nowhere in Luxor. Do you realize you've just anni-hilated Unsullied Islam, this city's entire cell of the Holy Voice?"

"Where the next-closest cell?"

"Cairo," she said somewhat breathlessly, trying to keep up with the soldier's rapid pace.

Bolan spotted a small, boxy car on the street and headed for it. It was a Fiat, a decade old. He reached under the rubber seal of the driver-side window and gripped the top of the glass, forcing it down into the door with little effort. Then he simply unlocked it and got in, opening the other door for his companion.

She stood outside staring in incredulously. "What are you planning to do, push us to Cairo with your feet out the door?"

Bolan was already under the dashboard, extracting wires. He used wire cutters from his backpack to cut them and remove insulation. Within a minute he had sparked them together. The Fiat sputtered to life.

"Let's go."

Ara got in, looking wildly around, fearing that the owner would suddenly appear. But the street remained deserted. She closed her door, and they left the street behind.

She guided him quickly to the main highway, which would take them north, more or less paralleling the Nile, through several smaller towns and eventually to Cairo.

"All right. We're on our way. Our benefactor even left us a full tank of gas," Bolan said. "Start talking."

"What do you want to know?"

"Everything. Who you are, what your relationship is to the Holy Voice and why you've come to me."

She nodded slowly as if trying to decide where to start. "My full name is Ara Emad," she said, then waited for Bolan's reaction.

"Kazem Emad's sister or wife?"

"His younger sister. And Abdul Assad's wife."

"I'm interested. Keep talking."

"When my parents died, almost ten years ago, I was just eleven years old. Kazem left the house, and I finished coming of age living with an uncle and his family. When he died, the family could no longer afford to take care of me, and I went to live with my brother Kazem a year ago.

"At first I looked up to him. I had heard about some of the things he had done, but in my family the truth was always filtered and he was called a hero. When I came to him, I believed in his sincerity and trusted him when he told me that his means were necessary to achieve the ends he desired.

"But when I came to him, I was also exposed to the possibility of true freedom for the first time. I came to believe that the ways of some of the most fervent Muslims were too harsh and restricting in their treatment of women.

"When I presented these ideas to Kazem, he disapproved. He beat me for even saying such things. They were blasphemous, he said. I was shamed into silence.

"And when Abdul Assad became tight with the group, with views that nearly matched my brother's, Kazem gave me to him. I was married to Abdul six weeks ago.

"I tried to escape and failed. And after I was married and after the marriage was…consummated, I felt bound to Abdul. I could not leave him then. To do so was to deny some of the basic precepts of my faith.

"But since living with him, I have been exposed to more outside influences—Western influences. I have felt myself becoming less a traditional Muslim and more and more believing in the rights of all peoples to freedom. And I believe that the law of my faith and this right to freedom do not have to be mutually exclusive.

"I never spoke out against the Holy Voice until I learned what kinds of activities Abdul and my brother were actually involved in. And I was with my husband when he went to Abu Simbel to witness the Holy Voice's first major strike."

Her voice had suddenly gone from pensive to stark and cold.

"I was there, Mr. Belasko. I saw the bus. I saw the bomber, strapped with explosives, board the bus and I knew what was going to happen. In that moment I knew how far Kazem and Abdul had allowed their hatred to overcome their humanity. I begged them both to stop it from happening. I told them God never gave men the right to kill innocent men. And they told me God never gave women the right to question the decisions of men." She swallowed, and a tear ran down her cheek. "I saw the bus explode. And all those people…

"That was when I knew they were truly evil men, Mr. Belasko. And when I overheard they were coming tonight to kill you, I took a taxi and followed them, just in case you managed to get away. And here I am.''

"Here you are," Bolan said. "The question is, what do I do with you?"

"You use me, Mr. Belasko. You use what I know," she said, tapping her forehead. "There is only one favor I ask in return."

"What's that?" Bolan asked.

"Spare Kazem. If possible. I know he doesn't deserve to live, but he is my brother. If you can save him..." She looked over at him. The soldier's expression was hard in the dim glow from the dashboard.

"I can't make that promise," he said simply. "If that changes your willingness to help me stop the Holy Voice, then let me know. I'll let you off right here."

Silence reigned for a moment.

"Well?"

"Keep driving," Ara said.

SALAH ABI SIGHED into the phone in mock annoyance. "You call at the most impolite hours, Mr. Belasko." He chuckled. "I'm actually most delighted to hear from you. I heard about a disturbance in Luxor this evening. Seems like someone did a nasty job on a bunch of suspected Holy Voice members. I was waiting to get the phone call telling me yours was one of the bodies at the scene. Next thing I know, you're calling me yourself. Good job."

"Thanks, but my news isn't all good. I'm afraid one of the Holy Voice members did escape. The one who set me up in that trap in the first place—Abdul Assad."

"No! He is sympathetic to the terrorists?"

"It appears he was all along. He tried to have me killed twice in the past twenty-four hours."

"This is very serious."

"Here's another interesting piece of news. I'm now on the road with a young woman named Ara Emad."

"Ara Emad! Did you kidnap her?"

"She came to me. At the battle scene. We're heading to Cairo, where she says there is a very active and large contingent of the Holy Voice. She thinks that this will be the most active group now that the Luxor group has been iced. She claims she can get in and feed me information on their intended hits."

"Do you trust her?"

"No, not yet."

"Be careful. She may be leading you into another trap. In fact, I'm sure she will."

"You may be right. But I'll chance it. If she's sincere about helping to stop the Holy Voice, it's an opportunity I can't afford to let slip through my fingers. I'll need help from you. Equipment." Bolan gave Abi a short list of hardware and armament.

"Yes, yes, this shouldn't be too difficult to round up. I'll have it waiting for you at International Destinations. It's a front we've opened recently to run in Cairo. It operates as a travel agency for English-speaking residents and visitors to Cairo. Ask for Ragai Sabri. He's an agency man."

Abi added that the agency would be able to provide a safehouse for Bolan's Cairo base, more secure than any hotel he could hope for.

Bolan accepted gratefully and hung up. Minutes later he was driving north again. Cairo was still more than a hundred miles ahead.

THE COOL LIGHT OF DAWN filled the narrow streets of Cairo, and the city awoke slowly. First came the activity of some merchants and bakers. Men who worked the earliest hours began to stroll the streets. They all ignored the old Fiat parked in front of the small travel agency, except one man. He was a young Egyptian in a starched white shirt, a tie with a demure pattern and a sand-colored jacket. Bolan saw the young man peer at him closely, then look away, and his movement caused his jacket to tighten over the sharp lines of a holster against his ribs.

The young man walked past the Fiat and nonchalantly turned back. Bolan saw him checking the license plate, which seemed to reassure him. He approached the car, and Bolan got out.

"Ragai Sabri," he said, offering a hand.

Bolan took it. "Michael Belasko."

"Come on in."

The man unlocked the agency doors. Bolan followed him to the rear office, where Sabri began to key a code into the electronic lock on a steel-plated strongbox.

"I got word from Abi about your arrival. Hope you weren't waiting long. You made good time."

He withdrew a single satchel and placed it on the desk. "Please inventory the equipment."

Bolan did so. He found a small electronic bug and a receiving device. There were several 30-round magazines for the MP-5 A-3, as well as a supply of Magnum rounds for the Desert Eagle and a ring of keys. A small piece of paper was folded in the bottom of the satchel. Bolan read it over quickly, memorizing the addresses, key codes and phone numbers.

"The address is the safehouse. The phone number is for me. Day or night it will reach me," Sabri assured him. "I'll provide whatever you need, including backup, if I can. Of course, the more time I have to get men or supplies together, the better. Any idea what you'll be needing?"

Bolan crumpled the paper into the wastebasket and hoisted the satchel. "Just this, I hope. Thanks for your help."

Sabri nodded and Bolan exited. Within fifteen minutes he and Ara were at the safehouse, a tiny bungalow in a wealthy subdivision. A large, camel-colored brick wall surrounded the tiny yard, preventing passersby from looking at the little house. Bolan also considered the fact that anybody lurking outside couldn't be seen by the building's occupants. Then he spotted remote-activated video monitoring cameras placed at the corners, tucked behind the leaves of a palm tree.

The soldier keyed in the code he had memorized, causing the wooden gate to roll out of the way, and they drove onto the short concrete driveway. As the door closed behind them Bolan noted to his satisfaction that it was steel plated and reinforced, tougher than it first appeared.

They entered the house and found two bedrooms with four beds each, a kitchen with a table that was big enough for eight and a living room with a large, low coffee table. One wall held a bank of television screens displaying black-and-white images of the grounds. Bolan assumed the cameras were IR-capable. A bank of three phones included built-in recording devices.

He found a sophisticated alarm, with motion detectors placed throughout the grounds, which he activated while Ara was heating prepared meals from the freezer.

He inspected the bedrooms and assigned the smaller one to Ara. It was still large enough, designed to accommodate four people. She took the last of the four beds, the farthest from the door.

"I have never spent the night outside of the house of my relatives. Or my husband. It is a new thing for me, almost frightening."

"Independence is frightening. The key is to learn self-reliance, and reliance on others."

"That will be hard for me, I think. I have lost my faith in those on whom I have always relied."

Bolan nodded. He understood.

"Can I trust you, Mr. Belasko?"

He stared at her hard. "Yes. If you've been level with me, then you can count on my support. But I'm not promising it will be a safe road, Ara."

She nodded, drawing her knees to her chest as she sat on the edge of the bed, in what Bolan would have thought was a purely Western posture. "I know it will not be safe. But faith—in God and in others—can carry us through danger."

Bolan wondered how true that statement was. He had witnessed more examples of betrayal than he cared to recall. And he wasn't convinced by any means that he could even trust this woman, as helpless and afraid as she might appear.

He left her with her loneliness.

IN HIS OWN BEDROOM he found the panel and hidden television monitor he had requested. The agency had made quick work of installing it. Or perhaps there had already been such a monitor in place. He turned it on and watched Ara in her own bedroom. He put a tape in the small videocassette deck and pushed the Record button. If and when she got up, the motion detectors would alert Bolan. If she made any calls on the nearby phone, he would hear every word on his own monitor. Anything he missed would be on the tape, preserved for review as needed. He would watch her every move, hear her every utterance.

Faith only went so far with the Executioner.

9

The motion-detector alarm awakened Bolan that afternoon. After sleeping most of the day, Ara had risen and was getting dressed. Bolan dressed himself, then turned up the volume on the unit when she headed for her telephone.

She dialed quickly and spoke in Arabic. The conversation was succinct, and Ara remained expressionless.

She hung up and left the room. Bolan heard her open the refrigerator. He picked up his own phone and quickly dialed International Destinations. Ragai Sabri answered.

"Belasko here. I need you to translate something for me."

"All right, Mr. Belasko."

Bolan had an idea as to the content of the conversation he had heard, but wanted expert confirmation. He rewound the videotape and replayed it, patching the audio into the phone so both sides of the conversation reached Sabri.

"The girl asks for a Fati Hannah," Sabri said. "She gets him on the line and tells him she managed to escape from Luxor and get to Cairo. Now she wants to join up with the group again. She doesn't state the name of the group specifically. But she says she is alone and afraid. She asks if they know what occurred in Luxor. Her home was raided by police. She assumes her husband is arrested or dead but doesn't know for certain. They give her an address in Cairo and say all will be explained when she reaches them."

Sabri gave the address to Bolan carefully.

"Thanks."

"Certainly, Mr. Belasko."

Arming himself with customary care, he added the agency-supplied items to his backpack. He stepped into the living room and found the Egyptian woman, dressed in a traditional robe, eating at the table. She glanced at him with a worried brow.

"Good evening."

He studied her. Was there suspicion in her expression? Did she exude the odor of betrayal? Time would tell.

"Let's get going," he said.

BY THE TIME THE GATE rolled away in front of them and they were easing onto the street, Ara told Bolan about the phone call she had made. She gave him the address he already had.

"I told them I was on my own and asked them for any details on Abdul. They wouldn't tell me anything, so I don't know if he's alive or dead. But they'll take me in for now."

"Do you know them?"

"Muslim men aren't wild about involving their women in business or about showing them off, even to their friends. But I've met them. And I know their wives, of course. That's who I've typically associated with when they've visited Abdul. And from them I can get more information than one would expect."

"Good. The most important information I need is the location of any attacks the Holy Voice is planning. And if the Cairo cell isn't planning them, I need to know who is. I need the location of the other cells, as well as the names of the people who head them, and how many men are involved. Most important, I'll need to find the location of your brother and the mastermind, Nabil Aman. Those are the linchpins in the structure of the Holy Voice. They'll have to be pulled if we're to fully dismantle it and save a lot of innocent lives.''

She nodded grimly.

"Take this." Bolan handed her a small cellular phone he had appropriated at the bungalow. "Hide it under your robe and don't let anybody know you have it. Keep it turned off except when you want to use it. The buzzer is disconnected so it won't ring accidentally. Call me at the number etched in the plastic of the mouthpiece.''

Ara inspected the mouthpiece and nodded.

"This will be the only way we'll have of communicating," Bolan stressed. "Call me as often as you can, and I'll answer whenever I can. If I don't answer, the call will be forwarded to International Destinations and they'll take messages. They might know how to get in touch with me quickly.''

They stopped the car on a side street blocks from the rendezvous Ara had planned. She exited first, followed by Bolan minutes later.

The late-afternoon streets of Cairo were stifling. That section of the city was called Islamic Cairo, where the streets teamed with poverty-stricken people living in tight streets and narrow alleys. Yet, among the filth and destitution existed some of the finest Arabesque monuments and buildings in Egypt.

The population dwelling in Islamic Cairo in the later twentieth century had little money and few of the accoutrements common to Western life, few televisions or stereos. There was much grain and little meat on the table, and not enough social services were available. Sewage facilities, notably, were missing. The filth that ran in the curbs was rank, and the afternoon sun hadn't dried it, only fermented it.

Bolan was in a cotton shirt and trousers of common

Arab styling and wasn't immediately singled out as a foreigner by most of the people on the street, though a few gave him curious stares. He ignored them, keeping his steady-paced pursuit of Ara, who walked quickly along the buildings, eyes averted from the men she passed. Crossing several alleys and cramped side streets, she arrived at a small square. The market booths stood empty except where an elderly woman gathered up a small crate containing a single chicken. The sun was behind the buildings, and the air had cooled only slightly. Bolan came to the edge of the square and stepped behind a flimsy booth wall. From there he watched Ara move slowly through the square as if perusing merchandise no longer on display.

The woman with the chicken crate glared at her—perhaps she thought Ara was a prostitute—and stomped out of the square. She walked past Bolan, who slid back into the shadows, and never knew he was there.

The Executioner scanned the square for a better hiding place, hoping he could find a more secure spot for the stakeout. Then time ran out. Two men appeared from the other entrance of the square and approached Ara. She nodded and followed the men when they turned away.

Bolan rapidly considered another path around the square but decided against it. That would slow him, and he would risk losing them during the delay. He edged from his hiding place and headed swiftly through the open area, keeping to what cover the rickety booth frames could provide. But no one was lying in wait in one of the surrounding buildings; no shots rang out during the twenty seconds he was exposed.

The square's exit on the opposite side was between two squat buildings, and Bolan became extracautious. He gripped the hidden Beretta 93-R, ready to withdraw it from his shirtfront and fire with a moment's notice. Few men could match the speed of the Executioner's draw. But gunmen standing around the corner with automatic weapons already trained on the spot he would emerge...

Ara passed through, and Bolan followed a minute behind her. There was no trap, no gunman waiting for him.

Already half a block ahead, Ara's distinctive robe and her two escorts were visible.

The walk continued for another fifteen minutes down the same street, which became more desolate and dark. By the time the party reached their multistoried home crowded among the hundreds of other dwellings, the sun was out of sight and the slums of Islamic Cairo had become shadowy and dismal.

Bolan's pace slowed as he approached the dwelling, a brick box that couldn't have had more than four or five rooms, and yet might house several families. Lights were on in all the windows, and there were voices from inside, mostly female.

He walked as slowly as he could without arousing the interest of any slum dwellers who might be watching out the windows. It was entirely possible this section of the city was full of Holy Voice supporters, who would warn them of any suspicious activity. Passing by the home of the terrorist group revealed a single illuminated streetside window shielded with a dank cloth. The smells leaking out pointed to a dinner of spiced *fuul*. The building next door, sharing a wall with the Holy Voice's building, was dark. Without giving himself time to completely devise a plan, the Executioner took advantage of the situation and stepped up to the door. The lock and door were flimsy, and the bolt yielded to one of his flexible metal picks so quickly that an observer wouldn't have thought he was doing more than using his key. Then he walked into the darkened room and closed the door behind him, hand on his Beretta.

In the slivers of light filtering through the bare, flat cloth hanging in the window, he saw no one in the front room. He listened hard and detected no noises from upstairs. It was too early for the dwellers to be sleeping, Bolan decided. They had to be out. Flattening against the bare side wall, he heard again, muffled, the activity in the house next door.

The stairs were narrow and well-worn, and took him to a loftlike second level divided into separate rooms by a patchwork of material hanging from the low ceiling. He nudged through the curtain with the Beretta and found no one in residence on either side of the divider, though the untidy cushions and blankets offered evidence of habitation.

Ara's voice came through the wall. He recognized it at once. He went to the wall and found a spot where the mortar had crumbled away between the bricks and he heard the conversation seeping through it.

He made out the words "Luxor" and "Abdul" and guessed she was giving them her story about her escape when the police came to Assad's house, about her flight from Luxor and a lie she had devised about getting a ride with a van load of elderly women.

Bolan used the tip of the Ka-bar fighting knife to grind slowly at the mortar, further pulverizing it. He could only guess how thick the wall was. When the hole was about four inches deep, a tiny pinpoint of light appeared.

Bolan tried to make out the shapes moving beyond the little hole.

"What can you tell me about my husband? Please tell me he is not dead!" Ara was pleading to Fati.

"Abdul is not dead," he replied, "but he was the only survivor of the attack—and he is hurt badly."

"Can you take me to him? I must be with him!"

"I don't know where he is. When I spoke with Kazem, he said Abdul was on his own and was suffering from loss of blood. He couldn't risk going to a hospital. He was therefore going to get himself either to Kazem or to us."

"Is my brother nearby?"

There was a pause, and Bolan wondered if she was pushing her luck.

"No. And it would be faster for Abdul to come here. But we have no access to medical help for him, while Kazem might."

Ara said nothing for a moment. "Please," she begged. "When can I go to my brother?"

"He did not say. You will stay with us as a guest of my house until he sends for you, under the guardianship of my wife and her sister."

Again she said nothing, as if awash in sorrow and doubt for her hurt husband. "I see. My brother will be most thankful for your taking me in. I am sure I will be safe in your house, Fati. And the plans of the Holy Voice are going to continue?"

"It is left to us to carry on the work of the others."

"Good—"

"I will give you any news from Kazem or Abdul when I get it."

She was being firmly dismissed. Bolan heard her leaving the room.

Then he heard a squeak from below and the door on the first floor opened. The occupants of the house were arriving home and, if they were members of the Holy Voice along with their neighbors, they might very well be armed. At this stage Bolan didn't wish to risk detection, let alone a full-scale gun battle. He had to get out in a hurry.

But there was a job to do first. He pulled the tiny plastic bug from his pack. The unit was a plastic disk as big as a nickel, with a tiny metal screen on one side over the microphone. He depressed the tiny red button on the underside and positioned the device carefully in the hole he'd made in the wall. A large pinch of putty, from a package the agency had also supplied, packed the bug in place. Bolan smoothed out the putty, listening to a torrent of conversation from the new arrivals below—there had to be five or six people talking.

He heard the conversation of two women drawing closer. They were discussing something in an animated fashion, the Arabic flying back and forth between them so fast Bolan didn't think he would be able to get the thread of the conversation had they been speaking Midwest American English. He scooped up a small pile of the mortar crumbs he'd dug from between the bricks and pressed them into the putty. The result looked enough like the original mortar that it would survive all but the closest inspection.

The two women reached the top of the stairs as Bolan jumped to his feet and stepped to the other side of the room divider, where he spotted a window on the far side of the room.

Stepping quickly to the window, he looked down on a narrow alley running alongside the house. It was a risky avenue of escape; a pedestrian might appear in the street at any time. Heavy footsteps on the stairs made up his mind. The soldier swung out the window, and as if on cue, a young man appeared in the street. Bolan hung from the windowsill against the side of the building, feeling the blood forced from his fingers, waiting for the pedestrian to pass and listening to the arrival of the man in the upper level of the house. The man walked into the soldier's side of the room, where his hands were still visible on the sill.

The pedestrian hadn't noticed him and disappeared from the street. In that instant Bolan let go of the sill. He listened for a cry of alarm in the window above that would mean he had been spotted. His legs coiled like springs, and he rolled onto his shoulder and back to dispel the force of the impact. Then he flattened against the wall, in the shadows, still listening for signs of detection.

There were none.

Bolan walked to the street, scanning both directions. The pedestrian who had stalled him was disappearing around a distant corner. There was no one else in sight. He adjusted his disheveled shirt and stepped into the narrow street, just another Egyptian man out walking at dusk.

10

"International Destinations."

"Sabri? Belasko. You receiving?"

"Yes. We started getting a signal on your frequency about six minutes ago."

"You're taping, I assume."

"Affirmative."

"I need a transcription ASAP. I think the Holy Voice is planning something for tonight. Maybe within the hour. I need to know when, where and what kind of firepower to expect."

"Yes, I will call you back shortly."

Bolan was heading back to his parked car at a brisk pace. He made what had originally been a fifteen-minute walk in half that time, and was just reaching the vehicle when the cellular phone rang.

"Sabri here. I've got the target site. Kazem Emad has authorized the Cairo cell to use another suicide bomber. They indicate he's wired with the Holy Voice's entire current inventory of C-4 plastic, as well as dynamite. Their target is the Madelaine Restaurant at the Hotel Cairo Towers II."

"A tourist place?" Bolan jumped into the Fiat and started it up.

"Yes, at Tala'at Harb Street. It's a big hotel district and sees mostly foreign visitors doing high-dollar business in

Egypt, as well as wealthy tourists. It caters to some of the country's most influential guests."

"I get the picture. I'm on my way."

SABRI'S DIRECTIONS took him to the Hotel Cairo Towers II within fifteen minutes, and he headed into the complex.

He found himself in a large atrium lobby. The deep burgundy of the carpets, the machine-generated coolness in the air, the distant tinkling of a piano player gave him an instant picture of the hotel's clientele—this establishment specialized in extravagance.

He crossed the lobby, ignored by a group of dapper German businessmen sipping drinks around a low lounge table, and walked along a brick archway in the direction of the restaurant. He passed into a glassed-in hallway, some forty yards long. It was lushly carpeted, and its lights were set low enough to allow some of the stars, as well as the rather spectacular landscape of other nearby hotels, to be viewed as guests walked in air-conditioned comfort from the lobby to the hotel's most expensive eating establishment.

The soldier stepped into the restaurant and made a quick scan of the guests. The night was still young, and the place was only half-full. The maître d' glared at Bolan's attire and pointedly ignored him.

It would fill up soon. The Holy Voice would strike when it had a full house.

No one present appeared to be the suicide bomber Bolan was expecting. The few patrons seemed to be Americans or Europeans. The staff's neat red uniforms couldn't hide a substantial amount of plastique and dynamite.

The man Bolan was expecting would be in Arab robes that would hide the bulk of the explosives taped to his body. He wouldn't be wearing the stiff grin of a vacationer or businessman or the professional smile of the staff. He would have the grim expression of a man about to send his soul to God.

He planted himself in a cushioned chair and unfolded a newspaper that had been abandoned there. Above it he could see directly down the open glass hallway. To the right of it he could see the front entrance to the restaurant. No one was entering without being inspected by him.

After staring at the Executioner for several minutes, the maître d' approached. "Is there something I can help you with, sir?" He had a British accent, and his perfect politeness implied Bolan should leave the premises.

"I'm waiting for a friend."

"Ah."

He didn't have long to wait.

He spotted the Arab at the far end of the glass hallway, and every combat instinct in his warrior's body began to flare.

The Arab was in heavy black robes that were too long and dragged on the ground. He was middle-aged, gaunt-faced as if he had been malnourished all his life, and visibly uncomfortable, as if he had never been in surroundings like the posh hotel. But most telling was his fear and self-absorption. Sweat poured down his face, and his eyes were glazed. His lips moved in what Bolan took to be prayer. He held his arms awkwardly away from his body like a child in a bulky snowsuit. And he made his way slowly down the hallway as if he were having second thoughts.

Bolan waited until the other occupants of the enclosed hallway, a formally dressed French couple, chatting easily, passed him, and by that time the suicide bomber was in the middle of the passage. The soldier placed the newspaper on the floor next to the chair, standing and drawing the Desert Eagle from his hip holster in a single fluid motion.

"Don't move another inch."

The bomber was so distracted by what he planned to do he didn't notice the Executioner at first. Then his eyes seemed to change their focus from deep space to the formidable .44 Magnum aimed directly at him. His footsteps slowed.

"I said stop."

The terrorist stopped.

"Hands up high and open them." He gestured with the Desert Eagle and watched the man's hands go up. They were empty, the detonator nowhere to be seen.

Bolan took a step toward the bomber. The bomber lowered his right hand suddenly, and the Desert Eagle blasted in the same instant. The Executioner heard screams behind him as the restaurant patrons and staff became aware of the drama unfolding; a man who had just entered the walkway at the far end changed his mind and fled. The bomber yelped and stared at the mangled remains of his hand, then reached across his body with his left hand and fumbled awkwardly at a fold of his robe.

The Desert Eagle blasted again, and the bomber flopped onto his back, his gaunt face in ruins.

There was a screeching of tires in the nearby lot. A sedan tore from its parking space, swinging into the grassy lawn alongside the walkway. Bolan watched a figure with a machine gun lean over the hood and aim the weapon in his direction. He beat the man to the punch, swiveling in a Weaver's stance and blasting through the glass at the car. The crash of the .44 Magnum slug punching through the glass melded with the stuttering of machine-gun fire, which stitched a path through panel after panel of the glass. The panes collapsed in irregular sheets that littered the body of the bomber.

Bolan realized the machine gunning was intended to take out the wall of glass separating the car from the dead bomber. The vehicle had screeched to a stop, and the machine gunner on the roof was handed a bottle with a flaming rag sticking from the top. The soldier fired again, his automatic counting mechanism telling him only one round remained in the Desert Eagle. The shot penetrated the still-collapsing glass as if it were a waterfall, passed within inches of the car roof and drilled into the gunman—too late. The Molotov cocktail was airborne.

Bolan wheeled toward the restaurant, waving the Desert Eagle at the stunned onlookers. "Get down!" he bellowed.

The flaming bottle of gasoline shattered and splashed liquid flame across the glass hallway, across the dead bomber.

The Executioner grabbed the maître d', seemingly mesmerized by the sight, and flung him roughly under a table before collapsing behind the host's podium.

The bomber's body burned for a single second before the dynamite exploded, flinging a fiery cloud in every direction. Bolan pressed against the podium and felt it disintegrating into scrapwood, then, as the force of the detonation died, he flung what was left of it away from him. His head was ringing with the impact, and a hot wind rushed in his ears. A quick look told him the restaurant was a mess but wasn't burning out of control.

He stepped through the rubble into the stretch of lawn, holstering the Desert Eagle and bringing the Beretta into play.

The terrorists, at the end of the driveway, dumped the dead machine gunner to the concrete unceremoniously. They started to turn and Bolan crouched behind a parked car. They hadn't seen him, didn't know he'd survived the blast. They would have to get by him to exit the lot.

And Bolan wasn't letting them go anywhere.

They drove slowly past a row of cars, and he knew they were watching the dying flames, admiring their handiwork.

In a firm stance, the concrete warm against his knees, he leveled the Beretta and listened to the approach of the car. He fired once when it appeared, and the front tire suddenly collapsed. He fired twice again, flattening the rear tire. He stepped to his feet as the car lurched to a halt, and the confused members of the Holy Voice clambered out to see what the problem was.

The soldier adjusted the Beretta 93-R to autofire. Aiming at the first head that appeared in his field of vision, he held down the trigger, hitting the man in the temple, jaw and throat, punching him to the concrete. The man exiting the car on the opposite side found his wits when he heard the close-range handgun fire and grabbed at the assault rifle dangling from a strap over his shoulder. The Executioner stroked the trigger again, and three holes appeared over the hardman's left pectoral. He glared accusingly at Bolan as he sank to the ground, dead before coming to a rest.

The car had careened sideways when it stopped, and the driver's door was blocked by a parked car. The driver scrambled for the passenger side and suddenly found the nose of a 9 mm autopistol staring at him through the open passenger window.

"Hand me that. Slowly."

A glance in the rearview mirror told the driver none of his men was left standing. He cautiously handed the American his Browning BDA pistol, grip first.

Bolan took the weapon and stepped back from the vehicle, waving the man out.

Instead, the terrorist stomped on the gas pedal and yanked with his entire body on the steering wheel. The car lunged in the soldier's direction, and the Beretta drilled three rounds through the window. The fender bashed into his leg and knocked him to the concrete. But when he bounced to his feet again, as agile as a cat, Bolan noted that the rounds had found the driver, who now ceased to be a problem.

"...apparently suffered only minor injuries. The only deaths reported were those of the attackers. Reports are unclear, but it appears a single gunman engaged the suicide bomber and four other terrorists. Rumors at the scene of the bombing include the possibility that the gunman was an Egyptian antiterrorism specialist, though some eyewitnesses claim he was an English-speaking foreigner."

"Who is that?" Kazem Emad raged, jumping to his feet and stomping across the room to a table full of his finest men. "I want to know who that is and I want to know right now!"

His best and finest had no answer to give him.

"It's the same man who foiled our efforts in Aswân. It's the same man who wiped out our people in Luxor." The speaker was Nabil Aman, who sat on the sofa watching the news report without even looking up to acknowledge Emad's tirade.

"What? How could it be? Abdul, could it be?"

Assad lay on a cot against the wall, shivering and covered in sweat. His shirt was plastered to the bandaged wound on his left pectoral, where a large section of flesh had been shot off. The end of his hand had been layered with gauze. The germs that bred in the unchanged bandages had seeped into Assad's bloodstream, and a fever was raging through his body.

With great effort the man struggled onto his elbow and

squeezed his eyes until he was able to achieve some kind of focus on the distant television.

"It's the same man," he croaked. "It must be. Belasko."

"Why do you think so?" Emad demanded.

Assad's watery eyes glared at him. "An American? Who tracks our people down despite our best efforts? Who finds us no matter how carefully we guard our secrets? Who wipes out our armies single-handedly? It has to be the same individual. Some American—" he waved his good hand in the air in a gesture of futility "—madman."

"Madman!" Now Nabil Aman did turn away from the television. "What's mad about him? He takes some chances, but he's incredibly skilled. He knows the machinations of combat better than we do. He's not a madman, but a warrior, the likes of which we do not have."

"You're to blame for that. You're here to train these men and you haven't! All you've offered is plans that get us killed," Emad stated.

"I'm the most skilled terror strategist in the Islamic world," Aman retorted quietly. "My plans would work if your men could carry them off in an efficient manner, and could keep silent beforehand. Besides, even I have never run up against opposition like this."

Assad collapsed onto his back and stared at the ceiling, mumbling.

"We should strike again soon," Aman said, rising from the couch and stepping close to Emad. "This time we should strike without advance warning, even to our own people. This American has methods of learning what our plans are, but this time we will thwart those methods."

Emad thought about it for a moment. Aman could almost see the wheels spinning. Then the leader of the Holy Voice turned to his men and waved briefly for them to leave. They filed out of the room and allowed Aman and

Emad to scheme in private, while Assad, fever worsening, sank into a quiet delirium.

"ABDUL!" ARA SAID the name in a terrified whisper and ran across the room to his bedside, where she held her hands above the semiconscious form as if afraid to touch him and yet desiring to embrace him.

At the sound of movement, she turned to her brother and stepped in his direction, then stopped. "Kazem," she cried, "who did this to my husband?"

"An American, the same one who has thwarted every one of our attacks since Aswân."

"One man couldn't have wiped out all of Abdul's men!"

"One man did."

Ara sobbed and turned to the sickbed again, looking at the ruin that was her husband. She could feel the dank heat radiating from him.

"Tell me you are not letting this man stop you, Kazem, that you will continue to fight."

"I will continue to fight. The Holy Voice will achieve its goals. Egypt will be God's holy nation."

"You will strike out at them again soon, the foreigners?" she asked breathlessly, turning to him.

Emad felt a smile on his lips. His little sister was the only person in the world who could make him smile any longer. "We will strike at them again, sooner than they suspect."

He saw the glint of excitement in her beautiful dark eyes. "Tell me," she pleaded, almost in a whisper.

AT TWO IN THE MORNING Bolan had been asleep just an hour. He had departed the Hotel Cairo Towers II before the emergency vehicles or media arrived, making his way to International Destinations. He wasn't surprised to find Ragai Sabri on the scene, watching the news reports.

"I was sitting here waiting to hear from you, but I see you handled it fine by yourself. You work well on your own."

Bolan phoned Salah Abi and gave him the full report, then obtained a secure line to Stony Man Farm.

"Many Americans in that restaurant, Striker?" Brognola asked.

"Several. I didn't count them."

"I know it doesn't matter to you, but it will be an assurance to the Man when it's learned that some of the lives saved were those of U.S. voters."

He returned to the agency bungalow for some sleep. The bruise in his side, caused by the car striking him, was beginning to throb, but he didn't lie awake letting it bother him. The next thing he knew, it was 2:00 a.m., and the cellular phone was ringing. He grabbed it in the darkness.

"Belasko."

"Don't say anything," Ara said in a small, frightened voice. "I'm taking a very big chance calling you. I'm in Cairo, with Kazem and Nabil Aman, but I don't know where. They've got an attack planned for late tomorrow morning. No one knows about it but the two of them and myself. They're going to a place outside Cairo called the Grayson site. I think it's one of those archaeology digs for tourists. They're going to hit it with all their men and automatic weapons. They've used up all their explosives and they're expecting another shipment in two days. That's all."

"Wait. Do you know where the explosives are coming from?"

"No!" Ara whispered. "And I have to go! Now!" The line went dead.

Bolan dialed the home number he had been given for

Salah Abi. The word that was spoken at the other end after several rings was indecipherable in any language, but at least the voice was recognizable.

"Belasko here," Bolan said.

Abi woke up and he switched to lucid English. "Belasko. What's up?"

"How soon can you get to Cairo?"

THE SOVIET-CONSTRUCTED Hip-C helicopter, on loan from Egyptian armed forces, roared 250 yards above the camp. Bolan made out a collection of large tents permanently erected on wooden bases. Numerous picnic tables were clustered near one end. A few hundred yards away the earth was scarred and discolored in large patches amid a grid created by wood stakes and cord.

"Grayson archaeological site," Salah Abi said loudly over the roar of the rotors. "It's not much. A few minor tombs and some sunken buildings. But it is authentic ancient Egyptian stuff, and the tourists eat it up. They come from all over America and Europe to be archaeologists for a few weeks. They get a crash course in the techniques, then they get to dig up pottery. Makes them feel like real Egyptologists."

Bolan nodded. "Any Egyptians here?"

"We don't come here. We're not very interested." Abi grinned. "Even the staff is mostly European."

"Sounds better and better from a Holy Voice point of view."

"Yes."

Behind him Abi's ten agency men were preparing their gear. Bolan watched the last of the inhabitants of the site piling into a bus under the direction of local police, who had been sent to the scene to escort them off the site. Abi's men were to replace them and act as decoys.

Bolan was taking a chance. If Emad and Aman were

trying to keep the site of the attack a secret, even from their own attack forces, until the last minute, then there should be no advance watch on the site. If there was a watch, then all this activity would scare them off. But it was the only way to move out the innocent civilians and establish an armed replacement force with such short notice.

The helicopter touched down, and the group headed toward the camp, squinting in the flying desert sand as the chopper took off behind them and immediately headed to a makeshift landing pad two miles away.

They entered the camp, which had the look of sudden desertion. Plates of half-eaten breakfast were on the picnic tables, and the smell of food drifted from the mess. Through the open doors of the tents, they saw unmade cots and clothes strewed about—some of the guests had still been sleeping when the police bus arrived a quarter-hour before and ordered everyone to quietly and quickly vacate the premises.

The plan was to dress as civilians and go about what would be normal site activities. When the Holy Voice arrived, they would find their victims had grown uncharacteristic teeth. Abi's men were well trained and well armed, most recruited from Egyptian army special forces. Bolan didn't doubt their abilities. What he worried about was their loyalty. Abdul Assad had also been a well-trained agency man, and now he was the enemy.

"Let's get into civvies!" Abi ordered, and his men headed for the tents.

MUSTAFA FARES WAS a bitter man. He had watched his father die in shame, an addict, in the gutters of the Cairo slums. Swearing he would achieve a level of dignity in his life that his father never could, Fares had struggled in a world that offered little opportunity. The hardships of a life of poverty left no room for school, no matter how much he sacrificed. The death of his stupid but industrious older brother, to some wasting disease that was never presented to a real doctor for diagnosis, left him with an extended family to support. He became filled with rage against the government that allowed men to live as he and his family lived. He had no one else to blame for his hardships.

Then Kazem Emad found him. Fares was easy prey, influenced like a suggestible child, exploited like a befuddled old man. Emad manipulated the youth's bitterness, and another Holy Voice loyalist was born.

And this day, Fares thought as he slapped the magazine into his assault rifle, he would be helping to make right the great wrong of the secular Republic of Egypt. He would help send a signal to the world that Egypt would not rest until it was made into an Islamic nation, God's holy nation, where *sharia* was the only law. He heard the words of Emad in his head just as Kazem Emad had spoken them to him, time after time.

But the image that burned in his mind wasn't that of a holy Egypt. It was of a convulsing, dying man, lying in the dirt outside the family's house in the slums of Cairo. Somehow the Western world was responsible for the dead man's addiction, shame and death, and today the Western world would begin to pay Fares back.

Walid Tawfik was driving the battered pickup, with eight men in the bed. They had removed their weapons from hiding beneath the blankets, and were now checking them for the battle to come. A van, with seven more men, was close behind. They were all veterans of the Cairo slums, Fares considered briefly. They all were owed some debt.

They crested a rise on the dirt road and ahead saw the green canvas tents of the Grayson archaeological site. The

debt was about to be paid, in part. A message was about
to be sent. The Holy Voice was about to speak.

BOLAN HEARD the approaching vehicles.

"Any air surveillance?" he asked over his shoulder.

Salah Abi signed off on the walkie-talkie, with which
he was alerting his men. "No."

"Good." Without an air watch, the approaching hardmen wouldn't be alerted that the camp-based troops possessed weapons.

"I've already ordered them to prep," Abi said. "Here
we go, my friend."

Bolan and Abi were stationed in the mess tent, hoping
that the attackers' vehicles would come into the camp
through the convenient opening next to it. But they heard
the vehicles veer apart. A pickup truck loaded with hardmen headed toward the dig site, where the agency men
were stationed, pretending to be tourists digging. The van
pulled in front of the picnic tables and halted with a sudden
squeal of brakes. Bolan stepped out of the tent as the van
door opened and men began pouring around the front of
the vehicle. His MP-5 A-3 was trained on them at chest
level when he ordered, "Freeze!"

The front man didn't do as he was told and raised his
submachine gun before him as a reflex action, and the
MP-5 A-3 stuttered quickly. The man threw up his hands,
flinging his weapon away, and fell to the hard earth.

"You're surrounded. Give it up."

The terrorists gazed mournfully at the corpse, then the
morning was shattered again, this time by the rattle of rifle
fire from the dig site, a hundred yards off. At that instant
another gunner stepped from around the back of the van
with his Czech Skorpion machine pistol leveled, and Abi
fired, downing the man before he had the chance to trigger
his weapon. Then the driver of the vehicle leveled a Mak-

arov PM and fired at Abi, who recoiled, falling back on his hands.

Bolan directed a stream of fire at the driver's door and saw the driver flop to the side, but the rest of the gunmen were diving behind the van.

"He got me, Belasko!" Abi shouted. His shoulder was covered in blood, and he was struggling to get to his feet.

"Stay down!" Bolan ordered, and sank to a crouch, squeezing the trigger on the MP-5 A-3 and taking out the van's tires. Then he fell on his elbows and blasted at the feet of the cowering terrorists. He heard the screams as they fell, and he continued pumping the 9 mm parabellum rounds into the fallen bodies. A few took flight, keeping the van between them and the subgun fire.

The MP-5 A-3's first magazine didn't last long, and Bolan left the weapon in the dirt as he sprang to his feet, grabbing at his newest acquisition, a mini-Uzi, strapped to his back. He took two long strides and launched himself onto the roof of the van, where he landed flat on his stomach with the mini-Uzi already triggering at whatever was still alive behind the van.

There were two Arabs on the ground, and one was out of commission permanently with massive groin and leg wounds. The second, wounded about the ankles and knees, shouted wordlessly at Bolan's sudden appearance and tried to make use of his Soviet autorifle. The mini-Uzi spit a burst into his chest, and he was still.

One of the fleeing men had already reached the brush. But the nearest of the escapees was limping on a shot ankle and turned when he heard the mini-Uzi fire. Bolan had the machine pistol trained on him before he could make an aggressive move, and he stood helpless.

"Throw it away," Bolan stated.

"I will not surrender," the Egyptian replied.

"Your choice—surrender or die."

A shot from nowhere shattered the front windshield of the van inches from Bolan's body, and he dragged himself forward off the top of the van, landing across the two corpses and instantly bringing the mini-Uzi back into play. He knew the man with the wounded foot would take the opportunity to use his assault rifle, and Bolan fired before he had the man clearly sighted. The weapon rattled in the terrorist's grip and stitched the van door inches above the soldier's head before the rounds from the mini-Uzi exploded against his ribs and ripped through his chest cavity.

The Egyptian had made the choice to die, after all.

Bolan crawled over the bodies and peered around the front tire of the van for the gunman who had taken the shot at the windshield. He spotted movement behind a steel trash barrel in the middle of the compound. The gunman was a refugee from the battle at the dig site. Bolan didn't have time to worry about what was happening there at the moment. He unloaded a few rounds at the trash barrel and heard them hit with sudden metallic music, and watched the barrel bounce and vibrate.

He had to get that barrel out of the way and he needed a bulldozer to do it. He drew the Desert Eagle from its holster and aimed at the top lip of the barrel. The .44 Magnum blast impacted with a noise like a church bell and momentarily tipped the barrel into the man cowering behind it, where it started to roll to the side.

The hardman fumbled desperately for the barrel, aware he was suddenly exposed, then heard the second blast from the powerful handgun. He felt the ground slam against the back of his head and sensed nothing else.

Bolan stood and made a quick, long-distance assessment of the battle at the dig site. There were bodies in the dig and bodies littering the ground near the pickup truck, but there were gunmen still alive on both sides. It was impossible to tell which side had the upper hand. The Executioner was about to change the odds.

He slammed a fresh clip into the mini-Uzi and raced toward the pickup truck. The gunmen were unaware of him until the deadly fire began to strafe them. Two men crouching in the bed of the truck stood, trembling as if in an earthquake, then slumped into the bed.

A hardman with an autorifle crouching behind the rear of the vehicle found no immediate cover and decided to save his own neck. He raised his hands and dropped his weapon. "Surrender! Surrender!"

"Coward!" The shout came from the opposite side of the pickup, and the barrel of an assault rifle appeared long enough to fire briefly. The victim's head snapped sideways and his arms dropped, then his whole body collapsed.

Bolan triggered the mini-Uzi on the cab of the pickup and shattered what glass remained, but he could still see the nose of the assault rifle peeking out. The gunman stepped into view long enough to level the weapon, the soldier dived to the ground, while the 7.62 mm rounds burned the air where he'd been standing. Bolan scrambled across the dry earth on all fours to the truck cab, then got to his feet.

Mustafa Fares was suddenly facing the dark American through the cab of the pickup truck, then the mini-Uzi rattled noisily. Fares twitched as his body absorbed at least five rounds. He spit at the American, defiant to the end, then his body ceased to function.

12

Kazem Emad dismissed the survivor with a wave of his hand, then watched the man walk backward out of the room as if he were afraid of being shot in the back.

Shooting him in the back was exactly what Emad wanted to do. The man could have been the only survivor of the battle at the archaeological site by fleeing. He hadn't even brought his gun back with him. He ought to be punished for that at least. But Emad wanted to punish him for the entire miserable failure.

"You know it was her," Aman said. "No one else knew."

"It could have been Abdul."

"Abdul was delirious. Even if he was motivated to be disloyal—and he's never exhibited such disloyalty—he wouldn't have had the strength to pick up a telephone."

"It could have been you."

Aman was a short, heavy man, with a round face, a thin beard and round eyes, almost boyish. But when he took a single step in the direction of Emad's desk, with his hands behind his back, the leader of the Holy Voice felt anger radiating from him like heat from a sunbaked boulder.

"I will ignore what you've said because I know you are only trying to protect your family and your mind is desperate to come up with any excuse to exonerate Ara. But you know she is guilty. She was the only other person who knew that today's attack was even going to happen, let alone its location. And you know she has expressed outrage with me and with the methods I am teaching the Holy Voice. Kazem, we lost fifteen more men today, lost them through treason. Someone must pay for this."

"I know." Emad nodded slightly. "I know."

"Where is she?"

"She took Abdul to the house of my cousin, Walid Tawfik. She said she wanted to take him to a house with women who could care for him."

"But we know now that she went to a place where she might communicate with the outside, with this agency man, Belasko, and the traitors to Islam who are his allies. And today, as a result of her betrayal, your cousin, Walid Tawfik, is among the dead."

Emad looked up, Aman's words firing up something like conviction in his eyes. "Yes." He stood and walked to the door of his office, pounding on it. Several of his lieutenants entered the room, showing the shock of this morning's defeat and eager to act.

"Hassan, you know the house of my cousin Walid Tawfik. My sister Ara is there. She is the one who betrayed us today. Yes, it was my own blood." He spit the words. "Go there and bring her to me."

THE RINGING PHONE interrupted the meeting.

"I thought you'd want to hear this, Mr. Belasko," Ragai Sabri said on the other end of the line. "Your bug picked it up about two minutes ago."

Bolan turned on the phone speaker and listened closely through the imperfections of the recording. After a few seconds of silence, voices came through the hiss, arguing in Arabic. There were pleading noises and wails as if of sorrow from one of the women. Two men's voices were demanding and belligerent. Then the voices faded.

"Did you catch any of that?" Abi asked. He was trying

to put a shirt on over the big wad of white bandage covering his shoulder. "They're onto her. Emad ordered her brought to him and sent men to get her. The woman you heard was the lady of the house. Apparently her husband was a cousin of Emad's and was one of the men we took out of action this morning. She told them Ara was at the big market, Sayyida Zeinab. The men searched the house, then said they were going to go look for her."

Bolan was up and grabbing his backpack and the cell phone. "You know where that market is?"

"Yes."

"What are our chances of finding her first?"

"Slim to none."

THE MARKET SPRAWLED through a series of alleys and narrow streets on the south end of the city. The conditions would make a fire inspector weep: booths were tottering and makeshift and bursting with goods—produce, bolts of textiles, sacks of grains. Shoppers filled any open space in masses dense enough to inspire claustrophobia in a Westerner. The atmosphere was thick and hot, full of the smells of sunbaked fruits and vegetables and people, and the air was filled with a babble of voices.

The call had come during the drive through the city. "Mr. Belasko, I am in danger."

"We're on our way now."

"Where?" Ara asked.

"To the Sayyida Zeinab."

"How did you know where I was?"

"I'll explain later. What's your situation?"

"One of them caught up to me in the middle of the market. He grabbed me. As soon as I recognized him as one of Kazem's men, I knew they suspected me of betraying them. I started yelling and the people came to my aid. I was able to break free and now I'm hiding."

"Good. Stay there. You're right. Emad is after you."

"He's sent many men. I've seen at least three I recognize. They're bullying through the crowds trying to find me."

"Where are you now?"

"There's a stall in the northeast corner of the market. It sells cotton cloth. I am in the rear of the booth, behind a stack of bolts. It's not very good cover."

"Can you find anything better?"

"It's too risky. Kazem's men are everywhere."

Bolan instructed Ara to stay calm and stay low, and to stay on the line. They parked as close to the market as was possible, Salah Abi on the radio with his own surviving men, who were not far behind them and would be setting up a perimeter around the market.

"Still with me?" Bolan asked into the phone.

"Yes."

Bolan and Abi began to make their way from the south end to the northeast quadrant of the market, scanning the endless crowds for a glimpse of an automatic weapon or simply the determined look that might identify the face of a terrorist on the prowl. There was a sound like a startled gasp from the phone.

"Ara?" Bolan asked again.

There was no answer.

"They've got her." He looked about the sea of heads. She had to be in the vicinity. He grabbed the reed poles that made up the frame of a hutlike stall—one of the sturdier structures—and clambered to the roof. At an altitude of ten feet he viewed a wider panorama, and he searched for signs of struggle.

He spotted a man with a woman held against his chest while she flailed like a hooked fish. He could see only the back of her head.

"Abi!" He descended into the crowd again and began

to muscle his way through, to the left and ahead, hoping what he'd seen was really Ara. He caught up to the man, whose movements were hampered by his uncooperative burden. Bolan unleathered the Beretta 93-R, stepped up behind the man and pressed the muzzle of the gun in his side. "Freeze."

He froze. Ara slipped out of his grip and wheeled sharply, only then realizing who had arrived on the scene. "Mr. Belasko!"

"Quiet."

Her former captor sent an elbow flying back at Bolan's jaw. The soldier was an experienced fighter in close quarters and avoided the debilitating impact, firing the silenced Beretta before the Egyptian had time to rethink his strategy. The noise was slightly audible, but no one in the vicinity noticed it. Bolan grabbed the slumping form and sat him against the post of a nearby stall.

Abi arrived, wincing and holding his shoulder, and glanced at the corpse as Bolan arranged a fold of his robe to more effectively hide the bloodstain. Head nodding on his chest, the terrorist might have been merely dozing.

Abi spoke quickly to the old man in the stall and handed him a bill. The old man smiled broadly and nodded.

"Our friend can take a nap here all day as far as he's concerned," Abi said, taking Ara's arm. "Now let's get out of here."

Bolan took Ara's other arm, and they started through the crowd, but only traveled a few strides before Ara gasped. "Over there."

The soldier spotted him immediately, a figure with an intense expression, peering through the crowds with inordinate interest.

"Head down," he told her. They turned away from the figure and pushed in the opposite direction. A half minute later Abi glanced back.

"He's onto us, my friend!"

"You take her. I'll deal with him."

They jogged to the right again, putting a thatched structure between themselves and their new pursuit, and Bolan ducked into hiding. Two men glared at him as he stepped inside their stall, but he gestured for silence, simultaneously withdrawing the Ka-bar knife from a sheath on his hip. He watched through the spaces in the wall as the terrorist stomped through the crowd, and then Bolan stepped around the corner, colliding with the terrorist roughly. He inserted the knife neatly under his rib cage, cutting across in a quick movement, and withdrew it just as suddenly. With a yank on the man's sleeve, the Executioner turned him around and pushed him into the crowds. The man was holding on to his stomach and trying to breathe as he staggered away, but the blood was now pouring into his lung. Bolan knew he would probably drown within minutes.

The Executioner wasn't going to stay around to witness it. He had other things to do.

13

Bolan stood on the edge of the Sayyida Zeinab market as if standing on the shore of a vast ocean.

"Well?" Salah Abi was a pace behind him, fidgeting impatiently and grimacing with pain. The wound in his shoulder was just hours old.

"You're right. They'll spot us and avoid us. And we can't possibly stake out the entire place properly with five men. We'd need a hundred. We're wasting our time."

"Then what, my friend? Why not send my men to the slum house as I suggested? Abdul Assad may still be there."

"Yeah. Send your men to the house. They're not going to find anything useful. If they've abandoned Assad there, I imagine he's dead or too sick to speak. And the Holy Voice won't have allowed their families to remain, either, if they know anything. Which they won't."

"But I'll send them anyway. In the meantime what do you and I do? And what do we do with her?" He nodded toward Ara, who was leaning against the car.

"Let's go back to the house and map out the next step of our offensive on the Holy Voice."

"But we don't know what their next move will be or where they are."

"She might."

They headed back to the bungalow in Bolan's car, a

rental Mercedes with a little more to offer in performance terms than the Fiat had.

"Ara, you mentioned on the phone that your brother was bringing in more explosives."

He saw her nod in the rearview mirror. "Yes. He was furious at the waste of the previous shipment. His master plan depends on large-scale destruction, which means large-scale explosives. He wants to kill hundreds of people. He feels it's necessary to achieve his aims."

"You're sure you do not know where he is in Cairo?"

She shrugged. "They brought me to the place in the back of a van. There was a window, but I was busy nursing Abdul and I didn't pay attention."

"Does he own any property in this city?"

"Not that I know of. And I have a feeling that after he learns I've escaped, he'll vacate the place anyway, in case I do know."

"I think you're right. So we need to concentrate on finding his source of weapons."

"He's an even sharper operator than I gave him credit for if he's been able to come up with another source for the kind of explosives we're talking about," Abi commented.

"Then you're giving him too much credit," Bolan said. "I'm sure he hasn't found a new source. He's just found a new method of transporting the explosives from his source into Egypt."

"I thought you wiped them out in Dalqu."

"I wiped out the distribution organization and the half of the shipment that hadn't made its way into Egypt yet. If it was paid for already, that means the source still owes Emad a substantial sum of money or another shipment of explosives."

"Well, who's this source, then, Belasko? Do you know?"

"Yeah. A Saudi, Satish Malkani, based in Riyadh. I learned about him about a week ago when I was on the trail of a load of heroin. Seems Emad paid for the heroin, which was to be shipped to Malkani in Riyadh, and Malkani would then send the weapons into Egypt via Dalqu, Sudan. Malkani has been branching into other illegal activities for a few years and has become one of the bigger suppliers of narcotics in Saudi Arabia. He engineered the deal."

"Innovative bartering," Abi commented.

"Yeah, but they ran into a few snags. I was onto Malkani's supplier and made sure the heroin never reached Riyadh. Along the way I managed to find out about the arms shipment going into Sudan and decided it would be best if it was neutralized. So Emad paid his money and never got all his explosives, Malkani delivered all the explosives but only half reached their destination."

"So Malkani still owes Emad half the supply of arms," Abi said, nodding.

"And since Malkani was the one who set up the deal, I'm sure he had to guarantee their delivery. He'll be taking a major loss but I'll bet he'll still be coming through with Emad's weapons. Malkani knows Emad has the potential to be a good customer in the long term, and he won't risk making him angry."

Abi grinned. "Good work, my friend. So we need to find out how Malkani will be sending his goods into Egypt." He looked at Bolan expectantly.

"We ask him." Bolan said.

WHEN THEY REACHED the bungalow, Bolan pulled a small notebook from his backpack and began leafing through it quickly. He found the phone number he was after and dialed it. Across the room Salah Abi was monitoring on a pair of headphones linked to the phone recorder.

Somewhere in Riyadh a phone rang twice and was answered with silence.

"This is a confidential call for Satish Malkani," Bolan said.

"Who are you?"

"My name is not important, but I have information that is vital to Satish Malkani."

"How did you get this phone number?"

"I used to be employed by one of Mr. Malkani's distribution supervisors in Dalqu."

There was a moment of silence. "I'm Malkani. Talk."

"I know who ripped you off, Mr. Malkani. I know who burned the shipment of heroin while it was en route to Riyadh. It is the same person that destroyed your other shipment in Sudan."

"You are right—I do consider this vital information. I'd very much like to get my hands on that person. What price for the information?"

"I'm selling this information cheap—thirty thousand Egyptian pounds," Bolan said. "One of the dead Sudanese was a personal friend and I would like to see his killer taken care of."

"You sound American."

"I am. But I live in Egypt. And I will need half the money delivered to Egypt before I give anyone the information. I will expect the other half of the money after you have convinced yourself that my information is legitimate. Sound fair?"

"Fair enough. It can be arranged. I have one of my top men in Egypt right now. When can you be in Cairo?"

"I'm there, in fact," Bolan said. "Where shall I meet your man, and how will I know him?"

There was a moment's pause. "Meet him at 6:00 p.m. this evening. His name is Gadish." He recited a street address. "I assume you will have some very convincing evidence as to the identity of this killer?"

"Very convincing, Mr. Malkani."

Bolan broke the connection.

Abi grinned. "We should have thought of it, Belasko—of course Malkani would be sending in one of his most trusted men to make this delivery, just to be sure nothing goes wrong."

Bolan nodded grimly. "Yes, but the fact that this man is already in Cairo leads me to believe the explosives are, as well. That means they may already be in the hands of the Holy Voice."

Abi's grin faded.

Before they left the bungalow, Salah Abi received two phone calls in quick succession. The first was from the hospital, where the two men wounded at the battle at the Grayson archaeological site had been taken. One had succumbed to those wounds.

"A good man," he said after ending the call. "A valuable man. The Holy Voice now owes me four lives."

The cellular rang again. It was the captain of his five remaining active agency men, checking in. The slum house had been found deserted. Assad hadn't been abandoned there, which meant he might still be alive.

Abi ordered the men to meet them at the rendezvous point, from which they would stage their next move on the street address given to them by Satish Malkani.

THE ADDRESS WAS A SMALL, locals-only café, little more than a patio on the street with a half-dozen tables. Bolan stepped under the roof, which shaded patrons from the sun but did little to keep out the oppressive heat of the late afternoon, and sat at one of the outside tables. He was in Western garb, obviously not an Arab, which earned him curious stares from the scattering of other patrons, any of whom might be his contact to Malkani. He ordered a bottle of Coca-Cola soda pop and sat sipping it, watching the traffic, letting himself be checked out by whoever might need to do so.

At six-fifteen he had identified the contact, although the contact didn't yet realize it. An Arab several tables away was glancing at him surreptitiously—or so he thought. Bolan was the expert at clandestine observation, and the man didn't realize that the entire time he thought he was spying on the American, the American was, in fact, watching him. After another five minutes of careful scrutiny, the Arab approached the table and said in English, "I believe we have an appointment, sir?"

Bolan looked up as if just noticing the man. "Are you Mr. Gadish from Satish Malkani?"

Gadish cringed at the obvious use of the names. "Yes," he said quietly, and sat down quickly.

"I've got this for you." Bolan pushed an unlabeled videotape across the table. "Have you got the money?"

A patron at the next table gave them a curious glance. Bolan's companion cringed again. "Please lower your voice."

"Oh. Sorry," he said more quietly. "Have you got the cash?"

"Yes. I have it right here. What's on the videotape?"

"A security camera took it in Dalqu. Mr. Malkani's transport chief was a friend of mine. I managed to get access to this after he was killed. It shows clearly who Osman's killer is. He even identifies himself."

"How do I know there is anything on this tape at all?"

Bolan shrugged. "Play it. I'll come with you if you like. We can look at it, and you can give me the money after you see it's legit."

Gadish shook his head. "No. Why don't I just take the tape and send you the money later?"

Bolan grimaced and pulled the tape back toward him. "Sorry. I'm not giving it up without at least half the cash, as agreed."

The Saudi nodded. "You're a shrewd man."

The soldier grinned, pretending to feel highly complimented, and pushed the tape forward again. "Here you go."

Gadish handed over a thick envelope. Bolan opened it with apparent greed and riffled through the currency.

"Good," he said. "I'll call Malkani in two days. You should have the tape to him by then? And we can make arrangements for the other half."

Gadish nodded and left the table without another word, taking the tape with him. When the Saudi had disappeared from sight Bolan left the café. When Abi's rented Ford pulled up, he jumped into the passenger seat and they cruised down the street after the Arab. The black Citroën filled with Abi's five agency soldiers was pulling from the curb ahead of them.

The voice of one of the men spoke over the radio. "See that beige Volkswagen Golf? That's your man."

The Citroën kept a careful distance behind the VW, and Abi maintained a safety cushion behind the Citroën. Bolan tried to make out the occupants in the VW and observed only a driver.

The VW kept to the tight, slow side streets of Cairo, avoiding the main thoroughfares, and the Citroën had to stay back in order to avoid alerting the driver to the tail. After fifteen minutes the Citroën traded the front position with Abi's Ford, so that, if keeping a close eye on the rearview mirror, the driver would at least be seeing a different car. The VW turned right up a slight incline, only a street lined with narrow but upscale town houses. The VW swerved into the short driveway and waited as the garage door started to open.

"Speed up," Bolan ordered. "Time it to drive past just when he should be bringing the vehicle to a stop inside the garage." He crawled quickly into the back seat and knelt on the floor, peering out the window with his hand on the door latch. Abi accelerated, then slowed as the Ford came parallel with the garage. The VW was just rolling to a stop inside the garage. Bolan yanked on the door handle, pushed it open and dived out of the Ford, hitting the pavement in a roll. He used his momentum to shoot back to his feet and run toward the garage in a crouch. He dived again, smacking against the concrete, the sound of the driver's door opening masking the sound of his impact, and he crawled quickly around the VW. As Gadish shut the door behind him and walked around the rear of the vehicle to get to the door into the town house, Bolan managed to keep the Golf between them. The garage door descended.

The Executioner sank to the floor and heard the door to the interior open and close, then the rattling of the garage door shutting, and he was in darkness. He waited for a full two minutes as his eyes adjusted.

There was a bright stream of sun peeking in the garage-door seams, and he used that to navigate through the narrow confines. It was a two-car garage, and Bolan took the time to notice that there was fresh oil in the empty space. Which meant there had been another car parked there recently, and that car might return at any time.

He stood on the single step and listened closely at the door, hearing what he took to be background noise coming from a small speaker—his contact had already put in the videotape. Bolan judged the sound to come from at least one room away.

With the Beretta in one hand, the soldier tried the knob and found it unlocked. He pushed it gently, opening the door just a crack, and peered into a small kitchen, windowless and unlit, but gleaming with new Turkish appliances and well-waxed ceramic tile.

Stepping into the kitchen, he shut the door and locked it, then quietly crossed the room.

The adjoining room was furnished with a low, plain couch and a stiff chair, facing away from the door, which was occupied by Gadish. He was staring at the television on the far wall, which was playing the video Bolan had sold him. The tape was actually from one of the security cameras at the Cairo bungalow. It showed only the outside wall, a section of the yard and a corner of the house. It showed six hours of absolutely no activity, but Bolan's contact didn't yet realize that. He aimed the remote at the VCR and fast-forwarded.

Bolan stepped into the sitting room and pulled heavily on the rear of the chair, sending its occupant flying backward into the floor, cursing and shouting.

"Don't get up," he said to Gadish, who found himself staring up at the business end of a 9 mm handgun. "No sudden moves."

"You. Who are you?"

"I'll ask the questions. I want to know where I can find the explosives intended for the Holy Voice."

"You surprise me. I was thinking you must be just a personal enemy of Satish Malkani."

"I am. But at the moment I'm more interested in the doings of the Holy Voice. What exactly is Malkani shipping them? When is Emad scheduled to pick it up?"

"I'll tell you nothing."

"Then your life is worthless to me."

"You won't kill a helpless man in cold blood."

"Why wouldn't I?"

Gadish thought it over for a second. "You're the one, aren't you? You're the one who killed Osman and destroyed Malkani's shipment in Sudan."

"I'm also the one who burned his shipment of heroin in the desert of Saudi Arabia."

"Then you have cost him hundreds of thousands of dollars in lost profits. Why would one man have such a vendetta against another man? What crime has Satish Malkani ever committed against you?"

"He's committed no crime against me. But he's perpetrated horror on the innocent people of this world. He's foisted drugs onto children in the streets of Riyadh. He's fed tools of destruction to the madmen of Egypt. In my book he's responsible for countless lives snuffed out or ruined."

"Then let the government of Saudi Arabia punish him," Gadish said.

"The Saudi government is a bureaucracy like every other government on the planet, and rich and powerful men like Malkani have their ways of navigating bureaucracy. But they can't escape me. I ignore the red tape, and I don't heed the rules of any society."

"So you're a killer. No different from Malkani. No different from me."

"Wrong. I'm an Executioner. And there is a difference."

The quiet house was filled suddenly with the thrum of an engine and the rattle of the garage door, opening at the command of a remote control. Gadish's companions were arriving home.

"Your time's up," the Saudi said.

"Stand up," Bolan ordered.

Gadish did as he was told, rising to his knees, then took his chance. He sat up suddenly, trying to punch Bolan in the groin. But the soldier twisted away at the first hint of movement, and his near-zero reaction time bought him escape from what might have been a debilitating blow. Gadish's fists slammed into the hand aiming the Beretta, and it was knocked to one side. The Arab launched himself off the floor, but the Executioner reacted with a swift knee that met Gadish's skull like a brick wall. The Saudi roared in pain and sprang again, but it was a fatal error. Bolan had been allowed the half second required to lower the Beretta and trigger it. The 9 mm parabellum round drilled into Gadish's forehead, through his brain, and he crumpled to the floor.

The silenced shot wouldn't have been heard, but Bolan didn't have time to move the body. He moved back into the next room, a small, bare office, and listened to the door from the garage open with a rattling of keys.

Bolan heard casual voices conversing in Arabic, and took the opportunity to trade the Beretta for the Desert Eagle, which would give him the stopping power he wanted, uncompromised by a suppressor. He heard a voice cry out in alarm, and chose that moment to reveal himself.

"Nobody move," he said, stepping into the open. There were three men: one stooped over the corpse, another behind him in the entrance to the kitchen and a third was in the kitchen. The man in the middle already had his auto-pistol out, and Bolan didn't know if it was a thoughtless reaction or simply stupidity that caused him to raise it. But before the Arab could aim, the Desert Eagle fired twice and punched him backward. The man in the kitchen ducked behind the wall for a fraction of a second, then just his hand snaked around the corner, holding a Glock 20 pistol. Bolan fired at the exposed hand, and the man screamed, somehow maintaining his grip on the weapon. He fell forward against the doorjamb, further exposed, eyes blazing with pain, and managed to will his shattered fingers to aim the gun again. Bolan's next shot spun him into full view, and the warrior fired twice more as the Saudi stood exposed in the kitchen doorway. The last bullet was a waste; the gunman was dead on his feet.

The third man, kneeling by the body of Gadish, stared at the Executioner with visible terror. Bolan placed the burning-hot barrel of the Desert Eagle against his forehead, and the man tried to watch it, going cross-eyed.

"I want to know what your shipment consisted of, where it is and when it is scheduled to be delivered to the Holy Voice."

The kneeling man was almost elderly and seemed to become more frail each second. "Malkani will kill me if I talk. If the Holy Voice doesn't get me first."

"Gadish didn't want to tell me, either."

The man glanced down at the corpse, then made a startled noise as the kitchen door burst open again and Salah Abi rushed inside, sweeping his Smith & Wesson pistol around the room until satisfied the danger was past.

"You're quite the mess maker, my friend," Abi said.

"It's about to get messier."

"No! I'll tell you anything!" the old man cried. "Just don't shoot!"

"No. You'll tell me *everything*," Bolan said in a low voice. "Or I *will* shoot."

14

Bolan wasn't at all sure that bringing Ara Emad to Alexandria was the wisest thing to do, but when he suggested she stay in Cairo under the protection of Salah Abi's men, she had refused instantly.

"I'm going to Alexandria, Mr. Belasko, whether you want me or not. And without me, you will never find the last family."

Bolan relented.

Ara had said she knew of only one more family group that belonged to the Holy Voice. Bolan had efficiently wiped out all the others. He had systematically destroyed the rungs in the ladder of families Emad had forged carefully up the Nile: Aswân, Luxor and Cairo. Alexandria was all that was left. "The Alexandria family is also the least organized and least trained of the Holy Voice families. Nabil Aman hasn't spent a lot of time with them, as far as I know. Kazem will only turn to them because the others have been neutralized," Ara explained.

"That's good news, eh, Belasko?" Abi said later on, when they were no longer in Ara's presence. "You've done exceedingly well. We've driven the rat to the end of the plank, so to speak. Now we push him off, and he drowns in the ocean. Or retreats into our trap."

"You've got an optimistic point of view, Abi. I think Emad developed his resources better than Ara knows, and I have a feeling that I'm not going to find much in Alexandria. If the family in Alexandria is as minor as Ara believes, and if Emad does have more to his organization than we or Ara know of, then my going to Alexandria may turn out to be useless.''

''But what else is there to do? Where else is there to go?'' Abi asked.

Bolan had no answer to give him.

DURING THE DRIVE to Alexandria, Bolan contemplated the information spilled by the old man employed by Satish Malkani. They had been unable to prove if it was true or a lie. Even if every word of it was true—and Bolan felt it was—it was still useless. It had got them nowhere.

The explosives had been dropped off earlier that day, and they had raced across town with Abi's gunmen to the drop-off point in Cairo. It was only an alley between two decrepit buildings. If an exchange of several hundred pounds of C-4 had been made here in the past few hours, there was no evidence of it now. The members of the Holy Voice wouldn't have been stupid enough to plan an exchange at any significant location. Now they had vanished.

Alexandria offered several advantages to the Holy Voice, Bolan considered. It was one of the most important Egyptian cities for visitors, and provided a wealth of possible tourist-site targets: the so-called Pompey's Pillar, the only Roman amphitheater in Egypt, the Catacombs of Kom esh-Shoqafa, the Tombs of Chatby.

Would Kazem Emad come here? His people here weren't as skilled as the families in the other cities, if Ara's judgment could be trusted. On the other hand, a suicide bombing required no battle skill. With the supply of C-4 Emad had now, he could carry out several suicide bombings, with the potential of taking out dozens or hundreds of innocent tourists. All he needed were devotees to his twisted vision of orthodox Islam.

Maybe Ara was right. Maybe Emad would be in Alexandria. And maybe Bolan would be able to track him down soon enough to stop him from voicing another "message" to the world.

He hoped so. If Ara was wrong, if the Executioner was leaving the Holy Voice behind to act out its schemes in Cairo unhindered....

The agency had no convenient and well-equipped bungalow in Alexandria. Bolan and Ara checked into a small but bustling hotel upon arrival, blending easily with the cosmopolitan clientele. They had driven through the night and arrived before dawn, then caught a few hours' sleep.

By 10:00 a.m. they were on the streets of Alexandria.

"THERE'S MAHMOUD." Ara said.

Bolan had already spotted the figure emerging from the shanty, squinting in the bright sun of the late morning. He was tall and dark, stooped almost as if hunchbacked. He was in his fifties, but his face showed the stress and ravages of a hard life spent in poverty. He gave Bolan the impression of being a petty thug, a man who used and abused everyone he knew and lived constantly in fear for his own safety.

A half-dozen younger men joined him in front of the flimsy dwelling and conversed among themselves. They all had the peaked look of the hunted.

"Those are his sons and sons-in-law. They all more or less work for him. They're engaged in petty crime, mostly, some protection and some thievery. That's what they did when Emad found them. And now they justify it with his doctrines. They believe they have the right to take what they want and abuse who they wish because they do so to promote their holy cause."

Bolan nodded. "It's an old story." Then he glimpsed the weapon one of the men carried under his robe. It was an automatic rifle. Petty thieves didn't typically need or have access to automatic weapons.

The soldier grabbed his backpack and stepped out of the car, keeping his eye on Mahmoud as he and his companions walked off in the other direction.

"You get back to the hotel and stay put."

"You'll never get at Mahmoud," Ara warned.

"I can try."

"His sons and sons-in-law are as dangerous as he is."

"I'll deal with them. Go."

Ara frowned and watched Bolan walk away, then drove off in the rented Mercedes.

Bolan felt noticeable as his pursuit of Mahmoud quickly led him through a poverty-stricken section of the city. They were as yet nowhere near any tourist sites. If the group was en route to a terrorist attack in the name of the Holy Voice, they had a long walk ahead.

Walk they did, several miles through the crumbling ruin of the Alexandria slum, past brick structures that might have been hundreds of years old but had none of the dignity of the historical places. The children played in the dirty streets. The unemployed men sat against the buildings and watched Bolan, curious at the appearance of a Westerner.

Mahmoud and his group emerged eventually into what was a less decrepit section of the city and crossed a major thoroughfare. Bolan, rounding a corner fifty paces behind them, was immediately drawn to an orange four-by-four with black windows, waiting at the curb.

There was a small café on the minimal sidewalk, and a man reading the daily paper. Mahmoud called to him. The paper was lowered and the man was on his feet, walking to the truck at once. The group headed directly toward it.

Bolan stayed on the opposite side of the street and searched for transportation. Mahmoud and his companions began to pile into the truck. The soldier knew he had less than a minute to come up with a way of pursuing them. He spotted a BMW R100 RS motorcycle with at least fifteen years behind it. The black leather was bleached gray by the sun, the twin tail pipes dented and utterly lacking the shine of chrome, while the rear springs were corroded. The engine was stained with baked-on oil deposits that might date back a decade. Nevertheless, the bike appeared operable, and it sat unattended on the sidewalk in front of an apartment building. He started quickly in the bike's direction.

When his quarry slammed the doors to the four-by-four and rolled down the street, the Executioner broke into a run and swung a leg onto the seat of the R100 RS. Yanking up the plastic cover, he found the bike's ignition system so covered in grease and filth he couldn't make out the color of the wires.

A figure stormed out of the building, shouting a torrent of angry words in Arabic. Bolan had just extracted the Ka-bar fighting knife to make a quick attempt at splicing the wires and hot-wiring the bike. The figure skidded to a halt, his curses dying in his throat. Gingerly he backed away from the soldier.

"I need the keys!" Bolan said.

Another, older man came out on the sidewalk and he, too, came to a sudden stop at the sight of the deadly blade. Bolan jammed the knife back into its sheath and ripped open the backpack as he dragged it from his shoulder, flipping a banded wad of bills at the irate owner. It was his take from Gadish and the foiled Saudi Arabian drug operations—enough to pay for a brand-new BMW motorcycle. The owner stared at the bundle in disbelief.

"Keys! *Mfatîh!*" Bolan demanded, pointing at the ignition on the bike. The older man seemed to understand.

"Mfatîh," he said by way of explanation to the younger man, who obediently withdrew two keys on a metal ring from his pocket. He held them out without taking his eyes from the bundle of bills.

Bolan grabbed the keys and jammed one into the ignition, searching the street ahead from the rear end of the orange four-by-four. The R100 RS roared to life and took to the street with a squeal of rubber and Bolan felt a moment of satisfaction. The bike retained more of its original performance than it had appeared. Accelerating smoothly, he weaved among the few cars that were on the narrow thoroughfare as if they were parked and glimpsed the truck ahead. He fed fuel to the bike. The 980 cc engine revved again, and the motorcycle tore through traffic. He was just in time to witness the rear of the orange truck as it turned right. Bolan took the bike around the same corner seconds later and decelerated slightly, giving himself a cushion of space behind the four-by-four.

They were heading west. The old, decrepit sections of Alexandria were left behind as they approached more developed areas. Well-maintained monuments dating to the city's founding still jutted here and there into the sky. Bolan spotted two buses crammed with tourists, mostly American and European, slowing to disembark at the Greco-Roman Museum.

Ahead of him the truck slowed, its occupants watching the tourists, evaluating their targets.

The occupants of the truck decided against the museum as their target, and drove a few more blocks before parking against the curb at the east entrance to El Manshiyya Square. From a study of a detailed map of Alexandria, Bolan knew that several major and minor streets and alleys let out onto the T-shaped square. The day was still young and the press of visitors still growing, most headed to the Tomb of the Unknown Soldier at the end of the square, stopping at the bookstores, markets, shops and stands along the way. The occupants of the truck emerged, except for the driver, and melted into the crowds. The vehicle drove away.

Bolan parked the motorcycle and followed. The group split into two at the intersection of the square, and the soldier went after the smaller of the groups—two of the men had threaded their way to the north of the intersection and now wandered through the visitors. One of the men was Mahmoud, the other a fierce-looking, bearded man in his late twenties. Both had the calm countenance of hunters as they perused the morning's crop of potential victims. They didn't yet know that today they were prey themselves.

Bolan had by now decided that there was no massive tourist attack pending. The mood was too relaxed, too casual. It was business as usual.

Mahmoud's first stop was at the edge of one of the wide visitor walkways where a merchant in brightly colored but old and ragged clothing was sitting in the middle of a large blanket strewed with trinkets, equally colorful. The man was scrawny, with a weary face, reminding Bolan, even from a distance, of a starving dog. He was selling a small plastic souvenir to a young Frenchwoman when he spotted Mahmoud. The smile he was wearing for the benefit of the woman faded. When she had completed her purchase, he turned his attention to Mahmoud, who made a cursory greeting and spoke quietly.

Thirty paces away, pretending to be engrossed in the scenery, Bolan couldn't make out the exchange. But the result was a passing of several bills—money he doubted the merchant could afford—to Mahmoud, who passed them to his fierce-looking companion. Then they went on their way. The merchant looked more weary than ever.

Bolan watched them turn into a narrow causeway, where a row of small booths was erected. Half the booths were empty. Mahmoud stopped at the first occupied spot and began his conversation with the merchant.

When the soldier walked close enough to listen in, the man was clearly begging for relief. Mahmoud wore a harsh grin, which didn't fade when he motioned to his companion, who stepped to the front of the booth and towered over the old man, putting a heavy hand on the merchant's shoulder so that he bowed under its weight. The old man pursed his lips as if to protest, then nodded slightly. He reached into his pocket and pulled out a green Egyptian twenty-pound note.

"Leave your money where it is," Bolan said as he stepped up and jammed the barrel of the Beretta 93-R into the young man's stomach. The old merchant stood looking with some confusion at the newcomer, currency in his fingers. Mahmoud turned quickly.

"Freeze, Mahmoud, or your boy gets drilled."

"Who are you, American?"

"Surely Kazem Emad told you to watch out for me."

Mahmoud's expression froze, and his voice was like ice. "Belasko."

"The same. Now I want to know where Emad is. And where his shipment from Saudi Arabia is being kept."

"How did you find me? Who told you where I was?"

"Mahmoud, I know where you live. I watched you leave your house this morning, and I've been on your trail all day."

Mahmoud's face had gone stern and angry. "And what do you want from me and Khalil?"

"As I said, I want to know where the shipment is that

came from Saudi Arabia, where it's being kept and where Emad is?"

"I know nothing about it. I haven't heard from Emad."

"I'm taking you down, Mahmoud. I'm taking in both of you. I'm having your family taken to jail—your wife and your children and your entire family. Then we'll see what you know."

Bolan had pushed the right button.

Mahmoud was now shaking with rage. His eyes blazed at Bolan and he spit out a single Arabic word that triggered Khalil into action. The young man yelled and twisted at Bolan, swinging his fist in the direction of his jaw with incredible speed. The soldier recoiled and fired, the Beretta firing once.

Khalil's roar became a bellow of pain, and he crumbled. Bolan leveled the gun at Mahmoud.

Then Khalil bounded back to his feet, launching himself at his adversary. Bolan triggered the Beretta again, without having to aim—his target was coming directly at him and absorbed the 9 mm parabellum rounds in midair, arms raised as if to crush Bolan in them. He staggered sideways, flopping to the earth at the big American's feet. One large hand shot out and snagged Bolan's ankle, yanking it sideways with amazing strength.

The Executioner hit the ground on his shoulder and back, but pushed down with his free hand, propelling himself back to his feet. He sought Mahmoud and saw only the man's back and heels as he fled.

Khalil pushed off the ground with a single hand and reached into his shirt, heaving against the pain, his torso and legs covered in blood. Bolan spotted the handgun and triggered the Beretta. Two 9 mm rounds cut into the younger man's brain, and he collapsed lifeless on the walk.

Bolan ignored the amazed look on the face of the old merchant and raced after Mahmoud, who had now disap-

peared—but there was only one way he could go. As the
booths were left behind, the walkway ran between two old
administrative buildings. The big American glimpsed the
barrel of a handgun as he approached a recessed doorway
and instantly flattened against the building. Twin blasts of
heavy-caliber fire echoed in the space between the buildings. The few pedestrians who had been on the street
quickly disappeared. Bolan aimed his weapon at chest
level.

"You're trapped, Mahmoud. Come out and tell me what
I want to know, and you'll live."

There was no answer from the doorway, but Bolan heard
footsteps running in his direction. He quickly adjusted the
Beretta to fire 3-round autobursts and directed his aim at
the open street. The first figure appeared. Bolan identified
him as one of Mahmoud's men even as he attained target
acquisition. The Beretta spoke, and the man toppled instantly with a leg suddenly and utterly ruined. His screams
warned his companions, and they never left cover.

There was movement from the doorway and Bolan targeted it next, firing three 9 mm rounds that knocked the
handgun out of Mahmoud's grip. He swore in his hiding
place.

Bolan reached the end of the building and ducked
around the corner after a quick check for more gunmen,
but found none. There was only a scared-looking Egyptian
businessman, who probably worked in one of the buildings
and who had been petrified by the gunfire.

"Get out of here," Bolan said, waving at him with the
Beretta. The businessman reacted by darting into the building via an aluminum service door.

The Executioner emptied the Beretta at the causeway
entrance, then fell back. That volley would hold them tem-
porarily. He holstered the Beretta and stepped to the door
as he brought out the Desert Eagle. He entered the building

and took the stairs leading up. Ascending two flights, he burst into a second-story hallway. A woman in a Western-style business suit ducked beneath the desk. Bolan ignored her, found another door and shouldered his way inside.

He was in a small office. The window was open, and a corroded and ancient desk fan sat on the filing cabinet, squeakily oscillating and sending a hot breeze through the room, rustling the loose papers on the desk. Someone cowered under the desk, but Bolan ignored him and stepped to the window.

He was almost directly above Mahmoud's hiding place. The street in front of the building was empty, but he made out Mahmoud's men, hiding behind the causeway corner. Bolan did some quick counting. There had been six men total. One had driven off in the four-by-four, and Khalil was dead. That meant Mahmoud and three others remained, one crippled.

One of the gunmen jumped out from the causeway and fired at the wall where Bolan had been stationed. A second gunman stepped into the open, laying down a suppressing fire at the soldier's previous position.

The Executioner leaned out the window, targeting the first of the gunners, and was spotted instantly. The man aimed his automatic at the second-story window, and there was a single blast. It didn't come from the automatic.

The first gunman fell onto his back, and his companion's head whipped to and fro as he searched for the killer. He saw nothing. The street was empty; the windows were empty. He hadn't seen what his companion was aiming at in the moment before he died. Shooting at the walls and street in desperation, he sidestepped in search of what he hoped would be better cover, then spotted a figure moving into view in the second-story window. He knew it was the gunman that had killed his companion, and he knew the man would target him well before he got to cover. He didn't have the time or the skill to make a preemptive shot. He was as good as dead.

The Desert Eagle spoke again and again, and the second gunman was flung into rotation and collapsed on his face just paces from his dead companion.

There was a burst of fire from directly below Bolan's window, from beneath the short overhang that shaded the front doorway from the hot Egyptian sun, but the rounds were wild, impacting the building far above his head. Mahmoud had recovered his handgun, but realized he was wasting rounds and halted.

Bolan stepped out of the window and onto the overhang, squatted, then lowered himself to a prone position on the ledge with the Desert Eagle pointed down at a spot just in front of the overhang.

Mahmoud stepped out, looking for Bolan in the window, and gasped in surprise to find himself suddenly inches and milliseconds from death. The soldier triggered the Desert Eagle, and Mahmoud's face shattered in the roar, a large chunk of his scalp flopping loose from his skull. He dropped.

Holstering the pistol momentarily, Bolan grabbed the edge of the overhang and dropped to the street next to the body. Mahmoud was no longer a threat. Making his way against the wall up the street he spotted the puddle of blood he was looking for—but it was bigger than he had anticipated. When he had shot the first assailant's knee, one of his rounds may have inadvertently opened the femoral artery, and if that was the case the assailant was no longer a concern. Following the river of blood took Bolan to the corpse, propped against the wall where the man had dragged himself in the minute or so before the loss of blood drained him of life.

The rattle of autofire filled the street, and Bolan fell into a crouch while directing the muzzle of the Desert Eagle on the source. He spotted the man who had been behind the wheel of the four-by-four. He had either stayed in close enough proximity to hear the gunfire or had been radioed by one of the other gunmen. His lack of skill with the weapon was evident in the erratic nature of his firing. He peppered the air with rounds and shouted in alarm when Bolan blasted the street next to his hiding place, one of the now-abandoned merchant booths. The return fire sent the gunman running.

He tore through the small market area, carelessly leaving himself open for a shot in the back. Bolan didn't take it but kept after him. Crossing the open El Manshiyya Square, he ripped at the door of the truck, which had been parked on the walkway in a hurry. He turned to Bolan in utter terror. The soldier made the most of it; he aimed at the ground a few feet shy of the truck and fired twice. The terrorist dragged at the gearshift, and the vehicle screeched over the curb, bouncing over a lane divider and into the street.

Bolan pounced into the saddle of the nearby BMW R100 RS and keyed it to life once again. The tires blackened the pavement as the motorcycle tore after the four-by-four.

The gunner was driving wildly, swerving across several lanes, eliciting honks of protests and shaken fists from other drivers. Bolan attempted to blend with the traffic without losing sight of the vehicle.

They went through town. As Bolan had hoped, the driver headed away from the Mahmoud home. Minutes later it became clear they were leaving the city of Alexandria.

The driver knew someone was watching the family. He couldn't return to his home. Mahmoud and the rest of the male members of the family were dead. He knew only one safe haven remained.

The Holy Voice.

15

When they left the city of Alexandria, Bolan increased his cushion behind his quarry. The traffic became lighter until, after forty-five minutes, they left the main highway and were the only two vehicles on the packed-dirt road. Now Bolan fell back almost a half mile, trailing the orange vehicle by the clouds of dust it left standing in the air behind it, and an occasional long-range glimpse.

They left the fertile delta at the northern tip of Egypt, where the Nile turned into a hundred small and great rivers, and came into the Libyan Desert. The clouds of dust became greater, the road became flatter, and the afternoon sun turned the world into a massive oven in which Bolan baked.

Then the four-by-four disappeared.

The Executioner had lost a gamble. He had kept as far back as possible, but the driver of the truck had still managed to spot him. And being the young, nervous type that Bolan assumed he was, the guy had panicked. He had gone off the road behind a dune. From the distance of his pursuit, Bolan hadn't noticed until too late, and he suddenly found himself without a dust cloud to follow.

He looked for tracks leading off the road, then dismounted and climbed up the highest dune and tried to locate any sign of the truck. After several minutes he admitted to himself his efforts were in vain. The driver had eluded him.

Bolan considered continuing along the desert road, but without knowing where to turn off, he could end up wandering the highway for days without any substantive lead. He turned the bike north again, back to Alexandria.

He had passed only a handful of automobiles and one semitrailer on the isolated highway. But the second car that roared by him when he started north caught his attention. It was the Mercedes he and Ara had rented in Cairo. And Ara Emad was driving it now.

Bolan was once again in pursuit.

ARA DIDN'T NOTICE HIM when she passed him on the road, and Bolan wasn't about to blow that advantage. He stayed almost a quarter-mile behind the Mercedes as it made its way through the desert, and half an hour later he saw it turn off and head seemingly into the middle of wasteland. He followed the woman on a hard-packed desert trail until he spotted a dark building rising on the far side of a distant sand dune.

A few palm trees and some tall grasses growing in shallow ravines told him the place was built on a tiny, isolated oasis. It was a sprawling compound, with a low central house constructed close to the water source and a four-bay garage to the north. A fuel dump a hundred yards northeast of the garage consisted of three large, above-ground tanks for fuel and a pump. To the south was an area of packed earth where an old dump truck sat, without tires and obviously nonfunctional. A collection of derelict earth-moving equipment littered the sand beyond.

Bolan killed the engine the instant he spotted the buildings, steering the motorcycle off the road and down a slight incline. Then he hid it behind a sand dune, where it was invisible from the road. He approached the compound on foot.

Midafternoon wasn't the ideal time for a soft probe, but

Bolan couldn't afford to wait for dusk to hide his approach. If he accurately judged the brains behind the Holy Voice, they would be itching to act. He wouldn't be surprised if they were planning to strike this day.

The Executioner was determined not to allow another Holy Voice act of terror to succeed.

Circling wide to the south took him a good five minutes, but allowed him to come at the compound from behind the dump truck, which prevented anyone in the main building from seeing him. The compound had a deserted look except for a pair of guards who flanked the rental Mercedes. It was the middle of the day, when the sun was at its hottest, and nobody wanted to be outside.

The sun had been glaring on the windows of the Mercedes. Now the door opened, and Bolan realized Ara had been inside all along. She was being allowed to exit now, but only because the two guards had been augmented by another four. All had their automatic weapons trained on her. A stocky, bearded man emerged from the front of the building, remaining in the shade of a short canopy, and watched the proceedings, his eyes meeting Ara's across the sand.

"Is this necessary, Kazem?" she asked.

Emad glared at his sister without comment. She stood at the front of the car looking uncomfortable.

An elderly woman emerged from the building, wiping her hands on a towel. She spoke deferentially to Emad, her head bowed. He gave quick orders that seemed to shock the old woman.

Emad spoke again, more harshly. The woman, mortified, approached Ara, who raised her arms and submitted to a patting down.

When the search was complete, Kazem approached her. Ara's hands remained raised at her sides. He snatched her keys and tossed them to one of the guards.

"Search it, inside and out."

Emad and Ara, under the close watch of the guards, retreated to the building.

One guard and Bolan were alone under the broiling desert sun. As the guard opened the rear doors of the Mercedes and started groping under the seats, the soldier launched himself from behind the shattered hulk of an ancient pickup and sped over the sand, distinctly aware of his vulnerability. Anyone watching from the main building or from the garage would spot him in an instant and pick him off with a single well-aimed shot. But he crossed the expanse of hard-packed sand and flattened against the wall of the building without attracting any attention.

The windows on the south end of the building were shaded. Nevertheless, he ducked under them to avoid showing a silhouette. The building had a back door that Bolan was tempted to try, but it was wooden and solid, and while he couldn't hear anyone beyond it, he couldn't be certain there wasn't a gunman just inside.

But at the end of the back wall of the house was a small stand of palm trees and a rare area of shade. A window had its blind lowered, but open. The tiny room was empty, an office of some kind. Bolan flattened his hands against the glass and forced the window up, listened for few seconds, then crawled over the sill.

The air-conditioned atmosphere was frigid against his heated skin. He closed the blind so no patrol would spot him, then searched the desk quickly and found nothing of interest. A few leftover scraps of official documents indicated the compound had once been an iron-ore mine.

Bolan fisted the silenced Beretta 93-R in hand, listened at the door and opened it cautiously. He heard voices, muffled. But one obviously belonged to Ara Emad; the other was her brother's.

"I've told him nothing!" Ara shouted. "He doesn't know I'm here!"

"You told him how to find my people in Alexandria, and today five of them died. Most of a family was wiped out, and you are responsible for it."

"Quite frankly, Kazem, I could not care less about the fate of the murderous thugs in your employ. But you are my brother and I don't want to see you killed."

"And why are you here?"

"I came to beg you again to stop. To halt the killing of innocent people, Kazem. It is evil work—"

Bolan could hear Emad step forward and slap Ara across the face.

"You who consort with my enemies come to tell me that my work—God's work—is evil? You who have abandoned God and his ways? You who dress like a man and talk like a man and don't have brains enough to stay out of man's way? I wouldn't be surprised if you've given yourself to him like some American slut."

"You have no right to talk to me that way!" Ara sobbed. "I came to speak to you in good faith!"

"I believe I've hit a nerve. It is true, isn't it? You've surrendered to your lust for the American, my enemy."

"No, Kazem!"

Bolan had by this time stalked down the short hall and stood at the entryway into what was essentially a large sitting area, and he peered carefully around the corner. There was an unfamiliar man on a wide, low couch, with a boyish face and a ragged beard, watching the proceedings with glinting, aroused eyes. Kazem Emad was standing a few paces away, towering over the prostrate Ara, his hand raised. He had just struck her again, knocking her to the floor this time, and she was sobbing into her hands.

"Have you led him here?"

"No!"

"Are you lying to me, girl? I'll kill you if you lie to me again!"

"I'm telling the truth, Kazem, I swear!"

She had raised her head, and Emad hit her repeatedly. The man on the couch shifted in his seat, and his mouth turned up slightly. Bolan believed he was looking at the engineer of the Holy Voice's campaign of terror, Nabil Aman.

"Get out of here. Leave my sight. Never come into my presence again. I say you are no longer a member of my family. I say you are nothing more than a diseased dog. Leave here now. Do us both a favor and leave Egypt. The next time I see you, I will kill you."

"Kazem, listen to me!"

"Go! I said go! Take her!" he ordered, gesturing to the far end of the room.

Guards appeared and grabbed Ara from the floor by the arms. She struggled to free herself, but they dragged her out a door at the other end of the room.

"What do you think?" Aman asked.

"About what?"

"Did she alert her consort, the American, to our location?"

Emad stood looking at the door she had been carried out, then crossed to a chair and fell into it. Bolan pulled back, outside Emad's line of sight. "I don't think she did, Nabil. I think she was telling the truth. She really was trying to protect me from him."

"But will she continue to do so?"

Emad didn't respond to that.

"Will she continue to protect you, as you put it, from this American?" Aman said again levelly.

"No. I don't think she will."

"Then what will we do?"

"Kill two birds, so to speak."

One of the guards returned. "She's left."

"Good. Take four men and follow her. Report to me when you've tracked her to wherever she is staying. She'll be with the American. I'm sure of that. Stake her out and kill him when he comes."

"What about her?" the guard asked.

"Bring her back to me afterward. We can't let her go free. I'll...decide what to do with her later."

"What about the balance of the shipment?" Aman asked.

"What about it?"

"Half the explosives are sitting in the city unprotected now that Mahmoud's gone. We should have it brought back here. These men can get it while they are in Alexandria."

"No. The risks of transport are greater than the risk of leaving it where it is. No one knows its location. But you're right in that we shouldn't leave it unprotected. We'll send guards."

"How many?"

Aman and Emad rose and crossed the room.

"I'm beginning to think even too many won't be sufficient," Emad said.

"We've underestimated this man at every turn. I'm thinking we're lucky to have been limited to just the damage we've sustained," Aman said.

"He's catching us with our guard down each and every time."

"We can't afford to let our guard down this time, Kazem. This time the shipment is in our hands, not Malkani's, and if it gets destroyed we are the ones who are out of the money. And I don't have to tell you we won't be able to come up with more funding on this scale in any short amount of time."

"That's where you're wrong, Nabil. Our next strike will

ring a chord of terror in the heart of the world, and will cause the hearts of the pure Muslims of Egypt to swell. Rich and poor. You will see. They will clamor to join us. And to fund our efforts."

The door to the room closed, and they were gone, leaving the Executioner alone with a few things to think about.

16

Bolan's strategy formed quickly. He had to neutralize Kazem Emad and Nabil Aman, and destroy their shipment of explosives. If he failed on either count, disaster would result. If only the explosives were destroyed, Emad and Aman would obtain more. If only the Holy Voice leaders were killed, doubtless there were devotees somewhere, whom Bolan might never be able to locate, to carry on Emad's murderous work.

Emad had spoken of sending nameless guards to watch over the shipment. Where these guards would originate hadn't been specified.

Bolan would have to force Emad's hand, make him panic, maybe make him believe his adversary already knew where the explosives were located.

That meant he had to convince Emad that his oasis compound wasn't a safe haven.

Half the explosives shipment was hidden somewhere in the city of Alexandria. Did that mean the other half was on the premises?

There was a soft footstep, and an armed Arab stepped around the corner. In his bare feet, without trying to, he had managed to get within a few yards of the soldier before his presence was detected. As it was, the Arab was the more surprised of the two. He started to speak and grabbed at a handgun he had tucked in his belt. The Beretta spoke before the weapon was free. The suppressed shot plugged into the Arab to the right of his sternum and punctured his lung. His eyes went wide, and he tried to inhale, making a desperate heaving noise. The second 9 mm round destroyed his heart.

Bolan caught the corpse as it pitched forward and dragged it into Emad's sitting room. He laid it behind the long, low couch and shoved it under the piece of furniture with his foot.

He retreated the way he had come, through the back hall and into the unused office. He crawled out the window on the west side of the building, then sprinted across the open desert to the gully, where the water was no more than a long, dark puddle in the sand, surrounded by scraggly weeds and grass. He tramped alongside the water, out of sight of the buildings, until he was closer to the garage.

The garage, not the house, would be the likely storage place for a serious cargo of high explosives.

The bay doors were closed, and the end of the clay-brick structure contained a single window with drawn shades. Bolan listened outside and heard the squeak of a radio station tuned in from Alexandria playing scratchy music.

Bolan opened the door and stepped inside, leveling the Beretta and finding only a single target within. An old Arab was slumped in a folding chair, hands on his lap, snoring. An AK-47 leaned against the wall next to him. The soldier stepped up silently and took the assault rifle.

The other door opened into the wide garage area. Bolan moved the crooked wooden door slightly and evaluated the occupants. Four men huddled around a backgammon board at the back wall, while a man in a grease-blackened shirt was lying under the front end of a dusty Chevrolet that was propped up on a jack. The game players' weapons were on the floor behind them.

At the far end of the garage sat a pile of boxes marked

with an Arabic symbol that Bolan couldn't read. He nevertheless recognized the same symbol that had been on the boxes of C-4 and dynamite he'd located and destroyed in the Sudanese stronghold.

The soldier stepped into the open and silently garnered the attention of the men playing the game. Their laughing conversation died to murmurs as they gazed down the barrel of Bolan's newly acquired AK-47, tucked under one arm, and the Beretta, silenced but adjusted to autofire, in the other hand. They raised their hands.

Bolan nudged the man under the Chevrolet with his foot. The man spoke in Arabic. When he received no answer, he rolled out from under the vehicle and found the Beretta staring him in the face.

"Go join your friends," Bolan ordered.

The man did as he was told. The soldier spotted one of the men gazing toward the weapons lying on the floor, evaluating the distance.

"Don't even think about it. Back up."

The men stood there.

"Back up."

There was a shuffle behind him, and Bolan whirled. The older man in the other room had turned out to be a light sleeper and was trying to sneak up behind him. The Executioner rapped the butt of the Beretta against his skull. The man dropped to the floor like a stone.

Bolan knew what to expect and turned instantly back to the group of game players. The foremost man had grabbed one of the AK-47s. The Beretta spit three times, and the Arab's gun clattered on the packed earth.

The other four men froze but were unable to take their eyes off the collapsing body. A groan escaped it as it shuddered on the floor and became a corpse.

Bolan stepped back and pushed the semiconscious old man with his foot, urging him up.

"Who speaks English?"

The old man rose on all fours and glared up at the soldier. "I speak English."

"Tell your friends to back up against the wall and to keep their hands in the air. You join them."

The old man spoke, and the captives obeyed. Bolan covered them with both weapons as he kicked their weapons away. Then he crossed to the gun rack and put down his assault rifle just long enough to systematically rid the rack of its weapons. Soon he had a large pile of guns.

The four-by-four he had followed from the battle with Mahmoud was one of the vehicles garaged there, along with a flatbed pickup at the far end and the Chevrolet. Since the four-by-four was the one vehicle he could be sure was operational, he intended to use it for his exit. The old flatbed truck also appeared operational. The keys were in the ignition, and Bolan started it just long enough to be sure it ran.

"This is the plan. You are going to load those boxes on the bed of this truck. You are going to do it slowly and carefully, because if I see any sudden moves you'll find yourself in the afterlife with your friend there. Understand?"

The old man translated, and the men nodded nervously. They approached the boxes, as much in fear of the explosives as of the big American, and gingerly started to lift them onto the truck bed.

Bolan heard a vehicle and looked out one of the grimy garage windows. A black car pulled into the compound, heading directly for the garage, its horn beeping.

"Let him in," Bolan ordered the older man, crossing the garage to the only available bay. "Act normal. Tell the rest of them to stay put on the far end of the garage."

The old man relayed the orders, and the others backed to the now-empty gun rack. The garage doors opened, and a Peugeot pulled in. The Egyptian at the wheel stopped the car and glanced at the four others.

"Out of the car," Bolan ordered, standing where the driver could see him in the side mirror."

The driver froze. "Okay, okay, I'm getting out," he said. He opened the door of the car with his left hand and pushed it wider, then twisted quickly in his seat with an automatic pistol. It was a foolish move. Even without a gun trained on him, he couldn't have achieved a decent target from his position. Bolan fired the Beretta, and the 9 mm rounds crashed through the glass of the rear window. One grazed the driver's skull, the two others piercing his head. Instead of dying instantly, he convulsed, triggering a shot that blasted into the packed dirt of the floor and filled the garage with sound.

As if poised to react, three gunmen erupted from the main house at the sound of the gunfire, charging toward the garage.

"You—back," Bolan said tersely to the old man, who retreated into the far corner with his companions. The Executioner aimed through the garage window and triggered the AK-47. There was no longer a need for silence. The glass shattered, and two of the gunmen were cut down by the 7.62 mm rounds. The third dived to the earth before he was hit and triggered his assault rifle.

Bolan stepped behind one of the brick supports between the bays and let the barrage of rounds from the weapon rattle against the garage door and pepper it with small holes. He waited for the volley to halt, then stepped into the window just as the last round hit the metal. He fired the AK-47 at the flat target lying on the earth—a difficult shot. But the gunman stiffened and went limp, letting his weapon slip from his hands and resting his face in the sand.

More gunners were emerging from the main house.

Bolan's sixth sense had activated again almost instantly, and he whipped the muzzle around to discover that the old man had made a surprisingly rapid dive for the stack of weapons. Instead of taking aim at the soldier, he whipped the small Ingram M-10 across the garage, aiming it at the spot behind the flatbed truck where the others were making a dive for cover. Only then did he make a grab for a weapon himself, bringing one of the AK-47s to bear.

Bolan cut loose with a burst, and the rounds cut into the old man's midriff, digging tattered craters in his gut. The soldier didn't linger to watch him fall but turned the weapon on the far wall, cutting a deadly swath into the brick above where the men were now squatting for safety. A figure appeared behind the boxes of C-4, holding the M-10, and took aim. Bolan fell to a battle crouch behind the Peugeot while the hail of .45-caliber rounds flew above his head, taking aim under the vehicles and laying on the trigger of the AK-47. There were screams as his rounds bit into feet, legs and knees, and above him Bolan heard the ricochet as the M-10 fire went wild into the ceiling. Then the AK-47 clicked empty.

The Executioner dropped it and sprang to the side, scrambling to the mound of weapons. He spotted the piece he wanted: a Barrett Light Fifty Model 82 A-1 sniper's rifle, firing the .50-caliber BMG cartridge. He checked the 11-round magazine and found it full. Now he was prepared to do some serious long-range damage.

First, though, he had to get rid of the nearby annoyances. He hoisted the Barrett onto the trunk of the Chevrolet, targeted the far wall, waited less than a second for a new gunman to appear, then triggered one time. The .50-caliber blast created thunder in the closed garage, smashed through the skull of the gunman and blasted through the brick behind him, creating a bloody porthole to daylight.

Then he crawled forward under cover of the nonfunctional Chevrolet and checked out one of the lowest windows, spotting five gunman on the prowl in front of the house, trying to get at the garage without exposing themselves. They weren't giving enough credit to their enemy. Bolan found the closest of the gunmen, trying to sneak up along the ditch into the pond, the same route the Executioner had himself used. He maneuvered the Barrett on its bipod, assessing the distance, and sighted carefully down the scope.

Maybe the man suddenly became aware of the vulnerability of his position; maybe some intuition told him death was standing at his shoulder. He started to run as Bolan fired. The .50-caliber round blasted through his shoulder, completely shattering the bones of the joint. The soldier fired again before the wounded man could fall, and the second round crashed into his chest cavity.

Bolan sought out others. They had chosen better cover—the vehicles parked before the house. But there was a lot of space between them and the garage. They weren't going to do much good there. The Executioner, however, had the skill and the hardware needed for just such a battle. He sighted on the narrow dome of one of the heads, waited for it to drift slightly from behind its shield, then triggered. The blast cut away a fist-sized chunk from the skull with surgical precision, and the man was dead on his knees.

Two of the other gunmen witnessed their comrade go down in a flurry of blood and took it as a cue. They stepped into view simultaneously, bearing down on the triggers of their submachine guns. Bolan retreated briefly and listened to the rain of rounds batter the garage doors, a few taking out the shards of glass remaining in the window, hitting the floors and walls.

Bolan's strategy was changing. It looked as if there was no way for him to make use of the C-4 shipment on the house, as he had intended. He could formulate no plan for getting it across the open area and to the house without getting himself targeted in the process. But he refused to leave without neutralizing it. If more innocent human beings were killed, it was going to be over his dead body.

He withdrew the only remaining high explosive grenade from his backpack and readied it. The HE had a ten-second delay. He needed to be sure of a secure withdrawal route before he activated it. At a lull in the fire, he rolled back to the window, intending to make the last six rounds in the Barrett matter. He looked for movement behind the vehicles and rode out three blasts from the weapon. The .50-caliber rounds crunched into the metal of the automobiles and at least one round found a target, judging from the shrieks of pain. Bolan was distracted by another submachine gun blast from the far side of the garage.

A third man had acquired the Ingram M-10, and one of them had to have had a backup magazine. He had waited for his enemy to reappear behind the battered Chevrolet, but the rounds bounced off the hood and sizzled in the air inches from Bolan's head and back.

The soldier lifted the big Barrett in the direction of the gunner and fired even as he was acquiring his target. The Arab's expression was almost comical at the sight of the massive, large-caliber piece maneuvering in his direction, and he ducked without attempting to make use of the M-10 again. Bolan triggered the remaining rounds from the Barrett into the wall above the heads of whatever survivors remained and put holes in the wall, allowing in shafts of the desert sun, which brilliantly illuminated the next missile Bolan sent in that direction. When the gunman poked his head up to fire again, he saw the small, dark metal shape of the grenade arcing through the air. It clattered among the wooden boxes containing the shipment of C-4 plastique.

Bolan dropped the spent rifle and jumped to the rear

door of the garage, falling against it with his shoulder and grabbing at the knob. It wouldn't turn.

The gunman desperately clambered onto the wooden boxes and found that his body blocked the sun. He couldn't see the grenade. He twisted to the side and allowed the shaft of light to illuminate the C-4 boxes.

Bolan drew the Desert Eagle while stepping back and fired at the locked doorknob, which transmuted into dangling scrap metal. The mental countdown in Bolan's brain was at five seconds, then six.

The gunman on the flatbed spotted the grenade where it had fallen between two boxes.

Bolan burst out the back of the garage. The ditch had made its way around the side of the garage, and he had assumed it continued behind the building, as well. He had planned to make use of it as cover, but the gully stopped. All he saw was flat earth.

Eight seconds. Nine seconds.

The gunman jammed his hand between the boxes. If he could just fling the thing to the other side of the garage, it might avoid detonating the C-4.... His fingertips touched the grenade but he couldn't reach it. He tried to force the boxes apart, scraping flesh from his knuckles.

Ten seconds.

Bolan dived to the ground.

The first blast of thunder was muffled, then was followed almost instantaneously by a rumbling that disintegrated the garage. Bolan was lifted and propelled through the air, his body flopping to the earth again as if he had been tossed like a toy. The force of the impact ricocheted through his torso painfully, then a chunk of clay brick walloped into his skull. Then the world went black.

17

He regained consciousness freezing cold, his mouth filled with sand, his face covered in it, his skull throbbing. He didn't move.

After several minutes the roar in his ears died to a distant rush. He lifted his head very slowly, letting the sand sift off it, and blinked his eyes open.

He was lying in the same spot his body had been thrown. The ruin of the garage lay around him in small pieces.

Night had fallen. The temperature had plummeted. The compound was silent and dark.

Bolan stood and brushed himself off, the movement sending shafts of pain through his back, shoulders and head. He found the Desert Eagle almost entirely covered with sand and brushed it off, but the gun would require dismantling and cleaning before being serviceable again.

Then he slowly crept across the open land to the ditch, where he sank into the weeds and carefully approached the house.

He suspected that the place had been deserted. Emad and Aman would have thought he'd been killed in the blast. His body had been covered and had to have been nearly invisible in the aftermath. And fearing that he had warned the agency prior to the explosion, and that reinforcements were on the way, they had vacated the premises.

That was the most logical conclusion he could think of. But he wasn't taking any chances. He entered the house through the same window he had used earlier in the day. He stalked the dark, silent halls for fifteen minutes before satisfying himself he was alone. Then he returned to the hidden motorcycle.

The icy desert air cleared his head as he made his way back to Alexandria.

What he would find in the city upon returning to his hotel would dictate his next course of action.

ARRIVING IN ALEXANDRIA just a few hours before dawn, Bolan stopped a block away from the small hotel where he had been staying with Ara Emad and parked the BMW R100 RS in a dark alley, next to a quiet building. He left his backpack with it, along with the useless Desert Eagle, but took an extra magazine for the Beretta. Then he approached the hotel stealthily in the darkness, silent and unseen.

The hotel was a grouping of four two-story buildings arranged around a small courtyard. The spaces between the buildings were narrow and the front two buildings were joined in the middle by a small lobby that faced south. The small suite Bolan had booked was in the west front building.

The Executioner approached from the street to the south and found what he had hoped to: the goon squad sent by Kazem Emad to keep watch over the suite, intending to snatch him when he returned. They hadn't received word from Emad that the man they were after had died in the explosion. Or Emad hadn't been sure it was the elusive American who caused the explosion and died in it. Either way, the stakeout squad was still in place.

Bolan found four men in a car on the street, looking directly up at the room. It took him just minutes to find the other two, peeking around the west end of the building. They were poised to be the first line of attack when the prey arrived.

The prey, little known to the gunners, was already on the scene, and had transformed itself into the hunter.

He circled around the east side of the building and slipped into the courtyard. He crossed through the palm trees and benches, seeking cover behind the low hedges during pauses in his recon, until he had come to the gap on the west side. He observed the two gunmen, one leaning against the building smoking a cigarette, letting a Colt Sporter dangle from his right hand, the other standing more attentive at the corner, watching the street. Both showed the boredom that was the result of several hours on a fruitless watch.

He stepped around the corner. The cigarette smoker looked up and was alarmed. The Beretta 93-R spoke quietly, and a triburst of parabellum manglers disabled the smoker's circulation system permanently.

The man on watch at the corner might have heard the discreet cough of the 93-R; he certainly heard the sound of the corpse's impact on the dry earth. He turned and witnessed the Executioner coming at him like a manifestation of death in the darkness. The Beretta chugged out three 9 mm rounds that ruined the guard's face before he could assess the situation and raise a cry. The soldier grabbed the corpse by the collar and yanked it from view of the car on the street.

He waited in the darkness. There was no reason the men in the car should have been alarmed unless they had been watching their man at the instant he was shot. Bolan was experienced enough to know such chances occasionally happen. He waited until he was sure there was no reaction from the car.

Then he waited some more.

The corpses possessed no radios, the men had to have been relying on staying in visual contact with their companions. It took fifteen minutes for the group in the car to realize something was amiss. Bolan peered around the corner unseen, and watched them open the doors. Three men stepped out, whispering among themselves. The driver remained behind.

They split up. Two headed to the building wall, then crept along it, heading toward the passage. The other gunner started down the street, tucking his autorifle out of sight behind him, making an attempt at playing the innocent pedestrian. Bolan wouldn't have been fooled even if he came upon the man by accident; his glance was too frequent and suspicious.

The timing was good between the man on the street and the two wall crawlers, however, forcing Bolan to act quickly if he wanted to take them out in the order he'd selected. He judged he had ten to fifteen seconds before the wall crawlers rounded the corner and spotted him, and his plan was to take out the pretend pedestrian prior to that. He stepped away from the wall, stooped in a battle stance and aimed across the street to the point in at the wall where the walker would appear. Three seconds later he did so. His last mistake was hesitating when he saw the surprising sight of a man standing in the open aiming a gun at him. If he had flung himself backward, the Executioner wouldn't have nailed him. But the triburst of 9 mm rounds, slowed by the sound suppressor and aimed in virtual darkness, homed in on him nevertheless. He turned to the right suddenly when the three rounds impacted his belly and hip, and dropped to the ground.

Bolan retreated into the courtyard and flung himself over the hedge. He waited for the wall crawlers to come around the corner, but they didn't. They'd spotted their downed partner and knew what was waiting for them.

The Executioner watched as dark, glittering eyes and the tops of heads peeked around the edge of the building. But now the distance was too great and the target too small. With a sniper rifle he might have made the shots, but not with the handgun. He chose not to fire until he could be sure of his kill.

The wait stretched into minutes, and Bolan was beginning to wonder if the gunners had decided to cut their losses and flee. But he maintained his watch, fore and aft, and spotted a movement in the shadow across the courtyard on the opposite side. One of the terrorists was using the same east entranceway he had used himself.

Then he heard the car on the street, backing up and approaching the opening to the courtyard. Its headlights swung into view, and the engine gunned.

Bolan fell to the ground and hugged the base of the hedge when the headlights suddenly illuminated the courtyard. The car roared through the narrow opening, scraping its doors on one of the brick walls, and screeched to a quick halt. The doors opened and two figures stepped out. They leaned on their autoweapons, blasting blindly at the trees, the hedges, the bushes, anything that might provide cover. Their shots were above the soldier, and the litter of slashed leaves snowed around him. The shooting lasted no more than fifteen seconds.

Lights flashed on in many of the hotel rooms, including the suite he shared with Ara. Now Bolan had reason to be concerned. He only hoped the guests would have sense enough not to come outside to see what was going on.

There was a slam of a door from the hotel lobby, followed by a shout in Arabic. Bolan swore softly under his breath. Some overprotective innkeeper was coming out to investigate. The soldier could no longer run this scenario on his own terms. Now he had to alter his prime objective from neutralizing the hardmen to protecting the innocent.

One of the terrorists yelled back. Through the branches at the base of the hedge, Bolan watched him wave his handgun, clearly ordering the innkeeper back inside.

The innkeeper shouted again, plainly enraged.

The handgun stopped waving.

Bolan aimed the Beretta between the branches of the hedge. The moment the handgun rose to firing level, the Executioner triggered a burst, downing the hardman, who thrashed on the ground screaming. The driver started to fire again, more wildly than ever, then paused. His eyes were shadowed, but Bolan made them out looking in his direction. He was spotted in his imperfect cover.

He had no choice but to fire again when the driver leveled his silver handgun in the warrior's direction. He wanted the man alive and able to talk, so he fired low. But one of the 9 mm rounds hit the bone in his thigh, exploding it. He fell to the ground in a slow writhe that didn't last long.

"Hama!"

The call came from the man on the other end of the courtyard. "Hama?" He was trying to get a response from his companions, but he didn't have any companions left.

Bolan rose into a stoop, surprised to see the innkeeper still standing at the rear entrance to the hotel lobby, a look of shock plastered on his face.

"Get inside," Bolan hissed.

The innkeeper's shock increased when he heard Bolan, and he tried to find him hidden in the foliage of the courtyard.

"Get inside!" Bolan slapped a fresh clip into the Beretta and changed the selector to single shot. Then he unloaded a round in the direction of the innkeeper. A five-foot-high picture window providing a scenic lobby view of the courtyard disintegrated noisily, finally snapping the innkeeper from his stupor. He retreated inside.

There was a blast of gunfire from the east entrance that struck the buildings and ricocheted away into the night. Bolan rose just long enough to send an equally wild shot in the direction of the gunner's shadow. That prompted another sweeping volley, which ended with a chug as the Makarov came up empty.

The shadow turned tail and fled into the night.

The Executioner launched himself to his feet, spun through the west entrance and looped around to the street, where he glimpsed the surviving gunman fly out from behind the opposite building and head down the intersecting avenue. Bolan sped after him. His nerves triggered electric spurts of pain through his battered body, but he ignored them, speeding around the corner and spotting the gunman far ahead. The terrorist tossed away his spent Makarov and glanced back long enough to see his would-be assassin a hundred yards behind.

Bolan let him think he was on the verge of escape, ducking into the narrow alley where the R100 RS was stowed. He mounted the vehicle, wrenched the handle mercilessly and felt the engine roar to life. He yanked the front end hard, twisting it in a tight half circle, and accelerated wildly out of the alley, bounding into the street. At full-throttle the 980 cc powerhouse raced to nearly eighty miles per hour within the space of a block and the fleeing gunman suddenly found himself targeted. He sprinted toward the sidewalk, intending to head for another alley, and Bolan homed in, the tire smashing into and over a parking curb. He twisted the bike to the left again, paralleling the building, compensating for the path of his panicking prey, and slammed his foot into the gunman's back. The Arab flew into the air as if tossed by a close-proximity explosion, then crashed to the ground.

The soldier rode into the street, swooped the bike in a tight loop and slowed as he headed for the gunman again.

The man was only just picking himself up, blood dripping from numerous cuts that covered his face and hands. A large red gash swept from his eyebrow into his hairline.

He tried to look up. Maybe he thought Bolan was going to run him down with the bike. The soldier slowed, grabbed at his collar, then accelerated with his free hand and dragged the man into the street.

"Where is the Holy Voice planning to strike?" he said loudly over the throb of the engine.

"Fuck you!"

Bolan released him and braked, watching the helpless form flop end over end before slamming again into the pavement. Like a large and half-crushed beetle he lay where he had stopped, his limbs moving slowly.

The soldier halted next to the prostrate man, turning him onto his back with his foot. The gunman's face was a bloody ruin swelling so quickly it looked as if it would pop.

"Where?"

"I will not tell. I am one of God's messengers."

"You are a cheap murderer and you're going to burn in hell for it. And it is going to be very soon unless I find out where the Holy Voice plans on using its last load of plastique and dynamite."

The gunman spit into the air.

Bolan spotted headlights a couple of blocks away.

"You've got a bus to catch, my friend."

Once again he grabbed the battered, bleeding man by the collar and accelerated, this time heading in the direction of the headlights. The gunman weakly pawed at Bolan's grip, then strained his neck when he, too, saw the headlights. Two blocks away was a ramshackle city bus, on its way to pick up early working Alexandrians.

Bolan headed for it.

"Stop!"

"Too late now." The soldier's words were grim and hard. The bus slowed when it saw the bike in the middle of the road, and the Executioner accelerated.

"Stop! I'll tell you!"

"Tell me. Then I'll stop."

"The *Golden Ibis!* A cruise ship for tourists! Two days from today!"

Bolan slowed slightly and looked at his victim as if considering his words. The man was craning his neck at the city bus, now less than a block away and closing fast.

"You're lying," Bolan said, and the bike shot forward again, the Executioner lining up to send the helpless man under the outside front wheel.

"It's true, I swear!" The terrorist twisted with sudden strength. "Please don't do it! I swear it is true!" The wail of his words was drowned in the roar of the motorcycle's soaring engine and the bellow from the horn of the city bus as it loomed at them, just yards away, when Bolan steered away from it, slowed and came to a stop at the edge of the pavement. His captive was sobbing and gasping for breath. By the time the soldier had tied the man's hands behind his back and dropped him in a patch of grass, he was hyperventilating.

Bolan snatched at his hair, yanking his head up, and the gunman's eyes went wide.

"If you lied to me, remember this, there'll be no place you can hide." The Executioner's diamond hard gaze left no mistake in the man's mind.

18

"Bad news. Your source told an untruth. There's no cruise at the time he said," Salah Abi declared.

Bolan said nothing, his mind spinning.

"I'm sorry, Belasko. There is a *Golden Ibis,* yes. It is a tourist boat, like he said, and it goes out onto the Mediterranean on dinner cruises, for the Americans and the Europeans out of the Western Harbor. But there is no cruise two days from now."

"Tomorrow?"

"No."

"Tonight?"

He heard papers being ruffled on the other end of the phone line. "Yes. Tonight there is a cruise scheduled."

"What time does it leave?"

"Six in the evening." Even as Salah Abi spoke the words Bolan looked at his watch and saw that it was 6:14 p.m.

"It's tonight," Bolan said. "I'm on my way there. Call and try to stop it from leaving if it's late by some chance. But don't tell them what the situation is. If they start a panic, the Holy Voice will know they've been found out and will blow the boat immediately."

"I've got it. We'll be right behind you."

The Executioner holstered the freshly oiled Desert Eagle and Beretta, and slung on the MP-5 A-3 subgun. His backpack had been restocked with incendiaries supplied by

Salah Abi. Two minutes after hanging up the phone, he was bringing the R100 RS to life, wheeling the motorcycle into traffic.

He hit the Corniche and roared toward the Western Harbor. He left the street, crossed a wide, paved loading area and spotted a large ship resting at the dock less than a block away from the Maritime Station. The roar of the bike sent dockworkers scattering and cursing as he raced toward it, then braked quickly, causing the bike to whine to a halt. There was a ticket office and a stream of what appeared to be mostly Americans and Europeans strolling under an entranceway to the boat, but the sign posted next to the causeway read *Cleopatra's Barge,* Dinner And Dancing Cruise. Departs 7:00 p.m. Returns, 11:00 p.m.

Bolan jumped off the bike and headed for the ticket window. "Where's the *Golden Ibis?*"

"Wrong place, sir," said a dapper Egyptian in a dinner jacket. "*Golden Ibis* is about a half kilometer that way."

Bolan jumped onto the bike and drove through the crowds and into the open area of the dock, accelerating in the direction of another well-maintained causeway with its own ticket booth. As he approached, he made out the name of the boat, *Golden Ibis,* on a marquee. The dock was empty. A large, well-lit craft motored leisurely through the harbor at least a half mile away.

There was every chance that the information he had wrung from the gunman that morning had been entirely fabricated. But Bolan didn't think so. In his gut was a feeling, borne of a warrior's sixth sense, developed over innumerable battles against uncounted foes, that told him there was danger in the evening air.

He gunned the bike, passing two large commuter craft before coming to a smaller version. It was a bulky nineteen-footer, with a large cabin that seated ten passengers. The engine rumbled steadily as it maneuvered to the dock, and a crewman hopped out with a mooring line. Parking the bike and killing the engine, Bolan jumped onto the deck of the ship.

The crewman made an indignant demand in Arabic.

Bolan entered the cabin, found it empty of passengers and stepped into the pilot's cabin. The Egyptian at the helm turned to him.

"Out," Bolan ordered.

The captain didn't speak English, apparently. Withdrawing the Desert Eagle, Bolan gestured with it to the rear of the craft, and the pilot understood, scrambling away. The soldier followed him and leveled the .44 Magnum pistol at the crewman, who had secured the line and was watching the fleeing captain curiously.

"Untie it."

The crewman did as he was told, then followed the captain down the dock.

Abi could offer them apologies later.

The water churned under the craft when he gave it full throttle. It lurched away from the dock, nose swinging to point in the direction of the distant cruise ship. The craft was small enough, and the engine powerful enough, to get it moving at a reasonable clip, and soon the shore was falling away behind.

The craft wasn't fast enough to suit Bolan, but it was at least faster than the cruise ship's current speed. The *Golden Ibis* was coming closer. Bolan made out figures on the top deck, while others lounged around the inside lower level, where it looked as if tables were set up for the dinner.

The Holy Voice wouldn't be planning to set off their explosives until the cruise ship was well out to sea, where they could be sure that many of the victims not killed in the blast would perish in the open waters before help could arrive. Kill as many as possible. That was terrorist logic.

Bolan wasn't going to let that happen. He intended to save each and every one of those people.

As he drew closer to the *Golden Ibis,* Bolan slowed to pace it. He couldn't come alongside the cruise ship without causing some extreme consternation among the crew and passengers—not to mention that his appearance would probably convince the suicide bomber to act prematurely.

The sun was approaching the horizon on the left, brilliant and pale in Alexandria's smog, shining like polished gold on the surface of the sea. Far to the right Bolan caught a glint of the light, as if on a diamond, and he spotted a low-profile speedboat. It seemed to have been heading north, as well, until that moment, when it turned and raced in the direction of Bolan's boat.

He quickly decelerated while scanning the surface of the bay for other craft—and he found it. Far to the left, equidistant from the cruise ship, was another, identical-looking speedboat. He had been expecting the Holy Voice to have some sort of a guard in place, not wanting to risk another failure.

He cut the engines. He needed to put as much space between himself and the *Golden Ibis* as possible before the other craft came near. Bolan was sure a suicide bomber was in place, which meant a man prepared to die, prepared to sacrifice everything. He would detonate himself the instant he thought his final mission might be in jeopardy.

The low-profile boat was a sleek, quick craft with a high-powered outboard motor. Four men were on board, and before they were within a hundred yards the soldier could make out the shapes of firearms in their hands.

Any doubt he might have harbored that this was a Holy Voice armed guard vanished.

MARWAN ESHAM STEERED the speedboat in a broad circle around the larger commuter craft, and passing around the front he saw clearly into the pilot's cabin.

"There's no one there!" Fayez Elabd said.

"Of course there is," Esham retorted. "We saw the motors get shut down. Unless he's drowned himself in the last minute, he's still on board."

"Then let's go take care of him."

"Be patient."

Esham slowed the craft as the circle was completed. "They're in hiding," he stated.

"They can't hide from four of us."

The speedboat came alongside the larger, bobbing ship. No sound came from inside.

"Marwan, what have you found?" The voice on the radio came from Ezzat Ashour, leader of the guard in the other speedboat, on watch on the western side of the *Golden Ibis.*

"A boat was approaching the target, and it came to a stop when we approached," Esham said into the hand-held radio mike. "We can't see anyone on board. We're going in to take care of the situation. I'll report back in a few minutes."

Esham opened his hand as if presenting the larger boat to Fayez Elabd. "You're right. They can't hide from us. So go find them."

Elabd looked nervous, then nodded. "All right. Come on," he said to the others.

He clambered onto the larger boat and over the cable fence that lined the outer walkways. He bent, then peered in through the passenger-cabin windows.

"I see no one. Let's go."

Elabd crept down the length of the commuter craft, awkwardly maneuvering the Makarov before him while his two companions crawled on board with him and crept behind. At the rear of the boat they peered into the cabin again before entering. Elabd saw Esham watching him from the wheel of the speedboat and felt foolish. He stepped inside the passenger cabin, sweeping the Makarov in every direction despite the fact he could clearly see there was no one to protect himself from. Just three upholstered passenger benches on either side, with enough seating space for nine passengers total. Several life jackets were piled on one of them, but nowhere was there room for a human being to be hiding.

Then Elabd knew. "He's hiding on the floor in the pilot cabin," he whispered to his companions. "I'll pull the door open. You two get him."

He stepped quietly to the door to the pilot's cabin and put his hand on the doorknob. His companions stood ready, both with Soviet AK-47 assault rifles. Elabd nodded, and his gunman nodded back. They were ready.

Elabd fled the door when he yanked it open, and his gunmen started emptying the boxes on the AK-47s into the floor of the pilot's cabin—then stopped. There was no one there. The tiny room was empty.

Elabd lay where he had flung himself, half sprawled on one of the passenger benches. Across the room he saw the untidy life preservers. At that instant he realized his mistake.

"Shoot the benches!" he cried. "He's hiding in one of the benches!"

The gunman rotated.

The Desert Eagle's boom filled the wooden storage area under the padded seat of the rear passenger bench, and less than two yards away one of the gunmen went down. The second shot brought down another. The third man yelled in fear and dropped to the ground. Bolan rose, pushing off the lid, and reached over the next bench to get a clear angle on the survivor.

Elabd brought his Makarov into play, firing it from the

floor into the ceiling while he was still attempting to sight the other gunman. Then he saw the head and shoulders appear from the storage area, the large handgun already aimed directly at him, and he knew he was dead.

Bolan triggered the .44 Magnum handgun a third time, and the Makarov dropped to the floor of the cabin.

There was a torrent of fire from outside, and the Executioner squatted as the cabin walls tattered around him. He peeked out the plastic window and spotted the survivor in the speedboat, standing at the helm with a Soviet RPK, fitted with a 75-round drum. He had unloaded a third of the 7.62 mm rounds into the wall and hull of the commuter boat, ripping it to shreds. Then he leaped behind the seat of the speedboat, powering it up and driving the craft into motion.

Bolan stepped out of the rear of the cabin and adopted a quick firing stance, aiming at the fleeing terrorist. He fired once, twice, and watched the pilot's head nod forward. The speedboat slowed and drifted to a halt.

The Executioner started the engines on the big commuter boat again and brought it alongside the speedboat, then anchored it. Unceremoniously he dumped the corpse of Esham on the commuter boat with his three dead companions. The last thing he did before appropriating the speedboat was to drag the long cotton robes off the least messy corpse and wrapped them around himself.

EZZAT ASHOUR STOOD in the other speedboat, bobbing on the sea. Ahead of him the *Golden Ibis* was nearly out of sight, but behind him and a mile away, the boat with Esham and his men was still parked next to the intruder commuter craft. He had heard gunshots over the noise of his own engines. Shouting into the radio was getting him nothing but hoarse.

Then the other speedboat started to move again, heading in his direction.

"What do you see?" Ashour asked. One of his men was keeping an eye on the scene through binoculars.

"I think there is just one man in the boat now. Yes, I'm sure there is just one man—Esham, I think."

The white-robed figure behind the wheel of the other speedboat waved with one hand and seemed to be holding something in it.

"It's his microphone," Ashour's man said. "I think it's not working."

Ashour cupped his hands. "What happened to the others?"

The driver of the second boat shook his head and steered his own boat in closer.

"What happened to the others?" Ashour repeated.

"That's not Marwan!" shouted the man with the glasses, and in that moment Ashour saw the stranger pull out a rifle and sit again at the wheel of the Holy Voice's speedboat, accelerating directly at them.

"Weapons!" Ashour snarled. His man was already scrambling for his Makarov PM pistol, which he whipped into position and triggered in pulses. Ashour heard the rattle of light machine-gun fire from the approaching boat. He leveled his own AK-47, triggering directly at the enemy. The pilot had ducked in the driver's seat and avoided their rounds, then spun the wheel hard, turning the speedboat nearly sideways in the water, sending it thundering within feet of the bow of its twin. The wake of it crashed underneath the terrorists' craft a second later, bounding it into the air, and Ashour had to grab at the wheel to keep from getting thrown out of his seat. One of his men fell facefirst to the floor, and the man with binoculars let go of his weapon so he could use both hands to hang on.

The other speedboat swung to a near halt.

Bolan brought the Heckler & Koch MP-5 A-3 into play. The driver of the other craft succeeded in triggering his Soviet assault rifle, but couldn't aim it while his boat was tossing on the wake. Bolan triggered the MP-5 A-3 and stitched his chest. The pilot dropped over the side of the craft, letting his rifle plop into the sea, and hung there, hands dangling in the water. Another man started triggering a 9 mm handgun across the water; Bolan cut through his shoulder and neck with another eight rounds from the MP-5 A-3. The other two men were on the floor of the boat and refused to show themselves. The soldier directed the steady stream of fire at the gas tank, emptying the subgun's 30-round magazine. The motor died, and a stain of gasoline began spreading behind the speedboat.

He withdrew one of the agency-supplied grenades from his pack and tossed it over the water, then sank into the seat of the speedboat and powered the craft out of there. He didn't hear the shouts of panic in the boat when the two survivors scrambled for the explosive, but he saw the orange flash in the rearview mirror when they failed to find it.

The *Golden Ibis* was a distant speck on the sea. Bolan was aware that every passing second was increasing the tension in the mind of the suicide bomber. He was unpredictable and liable to make his move at any second.

Bolan couldn't help but picture the explosion of the garage in the desert the night before. If that much plastique was set off in what was essentially a floating restaurant, how many innocent people would die at once? How many more would drown in the terrifying minutes that followed?

More importantly how was the Executioner going to keep it from happening?

He wasn't sure he knew the answer.

19

The *Golden Ibis* parked itself in the gently rolling waters of the Mediterranean Sea after its leisurely, hour-long trek from Alexandria. The American and European tourists crowded with drinks on the western rail of the top level and against the dining-level windows, watching the sun sink brilliantly into the ocean. Mack Bolan, peering through Steadyscope GS 982 binoculars, made a rough count and came up with ninety-plus. With crew and servers the number of potential victims topped one hundred.

The sea darkened quickly when the last brilliant shafts of pale sun disappeared into the sea. Bolan took the speedboat directly into the rear of the ship, the only angle he might approach unseen. He killed the motor and drifted in the last several yards, still not sure that the sound wouldn't be heard above the rumble of the ship's idling engines. On the bare outer hull, almost directly above the massive rotors, he spotted rungs set in the metal and headed for them. Securing the speedboat's line to the bottom rung, he stowed his backpack. The MP-5 A-3 would have to stay, as well. He pocketed only some extra magazines for his handguns, then started to climb up the rear of the cruise ship.

A small clutch of Americans was on the upper deck when he clambered over a rear wall and landed on the all-weather carpeting. They were sipping iced vodka or red wine, and were in dinner jackets and evening gowns. Their conversation stopped cold when the Executioner appeared.

"Where the hell did you come from?" asked a tipsy young man, whose accent labeled him a New Englander.

"That's the engine access," Bolan said, putting on a casual air. "It's for official use only."

The man seemed to want a better explanation, and was probably about to remind the soldier he wasn't dressed like a ship engineer, but Bolan left the group, focusing his attention on the mingling crowd.

A mental profile of the suicide bomber had formed in the Executioner's mind. It would be a male, Egyptian, and might be any age. He would be attempting to blend with the crowds, but in his eyes would be the determination and abandoned look of a man about to kill himself for a higher cause. He would exhibit some sense of uncertainty, because, unless Kazem Emad had utterly brainwashed him, he would have some doubts still. The burden of guilt would be on his brow, because no man could allow himself to be the instrument of holocaust, even if he had been brainwashed, without allowing some of the responsibility, however fervently denied, to hover about him like a black cloud.

It was for such a haunted figure that Mack Bolan searched.

And found more easily than he expected.

After covering the crowded top level, he descended the spiral staircase and stopped a couple of steps from the bottom, looking over the guests, who were already starting to gravitate to the tables for dinner, scheduled to begin shortly.

In the opposite corner of the room, seated at an otherwise empty table, was Abdul Assad.

Bolan continued down quickly, heading for the bar where the crowd was the most dense and would hide him best. But he soon realized he probably didn't have to worry about Assad, who was sunk deeply in his own thoughts. His brow was bathed in sweat, his eyes glazed. There was a pitcher of water on the table in front of him, already half-emptied, and he poured more into the glass and handled it awkwardly with one hand, downing it in a few gulps. The wounds he had received from the Executioner in Luxor days earlier were taking their toll.

Ordering a mineral water and sipping it from beyond a throng of elderly couples traveling from Chicago, Bolan could tell Assad was raging with fever. That meant he had received limited medical attention. From the wounds the man had received, Bolan was surprised he wasn't incoherent with heat and pain. Surely Emad wouldn't have allowed Assad enough in the way of drugs to stifle the agony of the wounds, for fear of making him sluggish.

In fact, Bolan mused, the pain and fever had doubtless been elements necessary to put Assad in the state of mind required to want to kill himself. Hopelessness and blind devotion to a cause were required for such a decision. Assad was too intellectual and sophisticated, when lucid, to decide such a course of action was a logical one.

The portrait was a terrifying one. Assad had metamorphosed from a simple traitor to a unpredictable, murderous, suicidal maniac. The Executioner would have to take him out quickly, quietly, without allowing the man even a moment's awareness of his presence. Because a moment was all it would take for Assad to trigger the explosives under his jacket.

He froze when Assad glanced at his watch and stood suddenly. Bolan reached inside his bulky jacket, hand on the Beretta 93-R, silenced and preselected to fire in automatic mode. Assad also put his hand beneath his jacket, then headed toward an Employees Only door. He didn't look around him. He was concentrating on the job at hand, his final duty. He had to remove his one good hand from his jacket again to twist the knob, and he pushed open the door with his knee, grabbing inside his jacket again as he entered.

Bolan placed his drink on the bar and strode quickly up behind Assad, without even allowing the door to close fully before he grabbed it and yanked it open, stepping inside and drawing the Beretta.

Inside was a door to the large control cabin and, to the right, a companionway leading down. Bolan heard Assad's steps descending. Now there was no crowd to panic. He would take out the man the moment he had an opportunity.

He raced to the companionway, just as Assad was entering another door at the bottom. Bolan descended in three leaps and yanked open the door, and was hit with a wall of rumbling noise from the engines. The terrorist was disappearing behind a giant, bulky section of the ship's powerhouse. The soldier walked around the engine, searching with the muzzle of the Beretta, and came upon Assad in a face-off with an engineer, who was standing before an electronic control panel. The gun in Assad's hand was a small, easily concealable .22-caliber weapon, but he was about to fire point-blank into the engineer's chest.

The Executioner achieved target acquisition on Assad's head, taking more care than if there been no innocent bystander. But the engineer threw a wrench in the smooth operation of the kill—he shoved at Assad in a desperate attempt at self-preservation. The terrorist was flung back against the hull, and he fired the .22 handgun three times. The engineer fell to the floor with a bloody wound in his shoulder, and the other bullets bounced with metallic noises off the pipes and flues leading into and out of the engine.

Bolan ignored the chaos erupting around him, but was aware of a flash of orange fire and a high-pressure spray of liquid from a ruptured pipe. Instead, he reacquired his target. Assad saw him, recognizing him, and clutched suddenly for the pocket of his jacket. The soldier triggered the Beretta, and a 3-round burst drilled into the terrorist's face, snapping his head back against the metal wall.

Bolan slid the Beretta into its holster and grabbed at Assad as he slumped to the floor, hoisting him into the air and onto his broad shoulders. He had no idea what type of triggering mechanism the Holy Voice might have installed on the man—it might require a coded input from Assad every few seconds to keep from blowing. It might be on a timer that was even now ticking off the few remaining seconds. And the soldier didn't have the time to stop to analyze it. He slammed through the door and bounded up the steps. A uniformed man was stepping out of the cabin with a look of alarm.

"There's a fire in the hull below. Help your engineer!" Bolan commanded.

He couldn't stay around to see if the Egyptian officer had understood him. He pounded out of the entrance, causing instant commotion in the dining room, and raced to the nearest companionway.

"Out of the way!" he shouted. Seeing the large man in black pounding up the stairs with a bloody corpse on his shoulders was enough motivation for the guests to flee. Bolan hurried across the deck and jettisoned Assad's body as he reached the guardrail, the corpse falling unceremoniously into the sea and sinking from sight.

20

Ara Emad glared at the two blank-faced guards standing at the door to the room.

"Am I allowed no privacy at all?"

"You are allowed to be alone in the bathroom," said one of the guards, who were Salah Abi's agency men.

"I can't sleep in a room with two men standing there watching me!"

"Sleep in the bathroom," the guard replied with a shrug.

Ara made a wordless exclamation of fury. She had been locked in the windowless, airless room for more than eighteen hours, ever since being picked up by the agency men, at the request of Mike Belasko, early that morning, just after he had incapacitated an attack force that had been waiting outside their hotel suite. She had been so astonished when he quietly accused her of betraying his confidence—and when he described her meeting with her brother, Kazem Emad, at his hiding place in the Libyan Desert—that she hadn't resisted.

"If you saw that interview, you know I was trying to get him to stop his killing," she protested when she had regained her composure.

"I do know. And I know you failed to convince him. And I know that if you had provided us with information on the location of the Holy Voice before now, they might be neutralized."

"You mean dead."

Bolan had showed no emotion. "Better a handful of dead murderers than who knows how many innocent people. Do you realize what he's planning now? He wants to take out a cruise ship. And I don't know if we'll be able to stop him. Can you guess how many people might be on one of the dinner cruises that goes out of the Western Harbor?"

Ara hadn't been able to reply, digesting this news.

"Dozens," Bolan said. "Dozens dead, if he succeeds, Ara. And at least part of the responsibility will be on your head."

He might as well have slapped her across the face. "No! I tried to stop him!" she retorted.

"If you wanted him stopped, you would have led us to him long ago."

"Can I be blamed for wanting to save my brother from prison or death?"

"You can be blamed for trading your brother's life for the lives of innocent people."

She had been unable to respond.

"And you won't have saved him, Ara. Because I will find him. Maybe I won't be able to stop his next attack, or even the one after that. But eventually Kazem Emad will fall to me."

NABIL AMAN STEPPED OUT of the taxi and looked up and down the sidewalk, then made it to the automatic doors with strides quite long for such a stubby figure. When he was inside the terminal, he found a seat with a view of the drop-off area protected by a glass case displaying advertisements for Alexandrian restaurants. He checked his watch. Two hours remained until his Gulf Air flight, two hours until he could escape this disaster.

He had been paid well for his expertise in strategy and

tactics, and the Holy Voice had learned well. But the Holy Voice had been too aggressive, its ambitions outpacing its abilities, and had brought ruin upon itself. Aman was now determined to get out while he could. He was booked on a five-thirty flight into Saudi Arabia, where he could effectively disappear.

An automobile with Kazem Emad in the passenger seat cruised slowly by the terminal entrance. Aman ducked behind the display case until it had passed, then got to his feet and headed through the terminal, his heart pounding. He knew Emad would want to pursue him.

But surely he wouldn't chance an open assault in an airport terminal. Nabil was unarmed—he knew better than to try to travel with a gun—and he felt naked and helpless.

He collided with a figure a full foot taller than himself and looked up into the face of one of Emad's men. Aman knew him to be young and stupid, and at the moment he was stupid enough to have carried a .38-caliber handgun into one of Egypt's busiest airports. He inserted the muzzle of the weapon in Aman's stomach just under the ribs, hard, as he put his free arm around his shoulders.

"Emad says I'm allowed to shoot you if I want to."

"What do you want with me?"

"Let's go."

The powerful man walked Aman to the door and out to the curb. Another of the cars belonging to the Holy Voice pulled up, and Aman was shoved in.

The driver glanced back and punched a number into the cellular phone on the dashboard.

"Yes, Kazem, we've got him."

SHE DID MANAGE to sleep eventually, fitfully, even with the guards watching her, until there was a buzz of activity throughout the house, which the agency had made its temporary headquarters. As she was waking, one of her guards was called away, and suddenly everything went quiet. She was aware that she and her guard were alone in the house.

"What's going on?" she asked him.

But he refused to tell her anything. She got the impression even he didn't know. It was hours before she heard the sound of vehicles returning, and there were other voices in the house.

"Is Belasko here?" she asked when a second guard returned to the room. "If Belasko is here, tell him I want to talk to him."

The guard left, and Bolan appeared minutes later.

"What do you want?"

"Tell me what's happened."

Bolan thought for a moment, looking hard at her, then dismissed the guards and sat in the room's one chair. "The Holy Voice placed a suicide bomber on a ship called the *Golden Ibis.* It sailed out of Alexandria West Harbor tonight on a dinner cruise with about one hundred passengers and crew on board."

"Oh, no! Don't tell me they succeeded!"

"They came very, very close. Their plan was for the bomber to wait until the ship was out on the Mediterranean, hoping that those not killed in the explosion would drown before rescue came. I managed to get on board and neutralize the bomber before he could detonate himself. He was the only one killed."

"Thank God!"

Bolan studied her carefully. He didn't trust her, although he couldn't help feeling her reaction was genuine.

"There's something else you should know. The suicide bomber was Abdul Assad."

Ara's face was expressionless for a long moment, then she looked at the floor. "He was my husband. But through no choice of mine. I didn't love him, even if I was some-

how emotionally dependent on him." Her voice dropped
to a whisper. "He got what he deserved."

Bolan stood.

"Wait," she said. "What's next?"

"That's a good question. Assad was outfitted with almost forty pounds of plastique, but I think that wasn't the
last of the Holy Voice's current supply. I'm betting they
decided to stretch out what they had left after I took care
of their stores in the desert. They mean to strike again,
soon. I'm convinced of that. But I can't even guess where
it will be."

Ara nodded slightly, biting her lower lip, her eyes fixed
to the floor.

"If you've got something to say, you'd better be
quick."

Her eyes were gleaming with a new resolve when she
looked at Bolan again. "I can help you find my brother."

THE CELLULAR PHONE on the dashboard rang, and when
Emad picked it up he heard his sister's voice. She sounded
as if she were weeping.

"Kazem, you once said all I had to do was call when I
wanted to come back to you. I am calling now."

"That was before you betrayed me, Ara," he answered,
his voice cold. Then it softened ever so slightly. "Why
now, Ara?"

"I have heard what they did to my husband. They mur-
dered my husband, Kazem!"

"Yes, Abdul is dead, Ara. And his last great work was
made meaningless."

She sobbed.

"He was snuffed out like a dog without dignity. And it
was your friend Belasko who is responsible."

"He's no friend of mine, I swear, Kazem! I hate him
for what he did! I hate him!"

"Then you come to me of your own will, Ara?"

"Yes! Come take me with you! They have me, but I can escape easily. I want to help you in your work—Abdul's work. I want to continue what he started, in honor of him."

She quickly rattled off the name of an intersection. "I'll be there in five minutes. You must come quickly. They'll all be back soon, and I must be away before then!"

She hung up the phone and put her hand over her eyes for a moment.

"Ara?"

"Yes! Let's go."

She had been quickly rigged with an agency-supplied short-range transmitting device, not on par with what Stony Man Farm might have been able to provide but good enough within about a quarter-mile. It was undetectable under her clothing. Abi's men were already waiting in one of the vehicles in the driveway. Abi and Bolan would lead the way in another car.

They left the house. Bolan stepped into Abi's car, and they watched as Ara walked to the street and headed for the intersection she had given to Emad. It was, in fact, not forty yards from the agency house.

"Testing," she said into her microphone, and the word came loud and clear from the receiver in Abi's car. He flashed the parking lights briefly in response.

"Somebody's coming," she added a few minutes later.

There was a pair of headlights, and a car drove past her, turned and pulled to a stop in front of her. She scrambled into the back seat.

"Kazem," they heard her say in greeting.

Bolan hoped she knew what she was doing. This was a dangerous, deadly game, and he was plagued with dread for her. Brother or not, he didn't think Emad would restrain himself from meting out the ultimate punishment if he realized she was setting him up.

The car pulled away.

The Executioner and his small army followed.

"It's been a hard time," Bolan heard Kazem Emad say. "This Belasko has shrunk our ranks drastically. And he's played me for a fool. He's managed to foil our attacks time and again. Who is he?"

"I learned only that he was an American sent in to help the Egyptian antiterrorism task force. I don't know if he is CIA or what," Ara said. "What will you do about him?"

"He doesn't matter anymore. I've got a last plan in the works. One he won't be able to stop. One that I know will succeed."

"What is it?" she asked.

"Don't push too hard," Abi said aloud to the receiver. Bolan had been thinking the very same words.

"I'm not going to tell you," Emad replied to his sister. "But I'm going to show you."

Bolan didn't like the sound of that at all.

Ara attempted to engage her brother in further conversation, but Kazem was sullen and quiet. They drove across the city.

"When can we take them?" Abi asked.

"When we know what Emad's got up his sleeve," Bolan said.

Emad's car pulled into the parking lot of the Alexander the Great Hotel, its white front illuminated with recessed white lights, its parking lot brightly lighted. A string of taxis waited at the lobby doors, arriving and leaving. Guests walked in the front garden areas of the hotel.

"This looks bad, my friend," Abi answered.

"It does."

Emad pulled into the small area reserved for check-in parking.

"What are we doing here?" Ara asked, her words clear over the receiver.

"You'll see, Ara," Emad answered. "I've asked my friends to meet us here."

"If Nabil Aman is joining him, we'll close in," Bolan said.

Abi nodded. "Right. But how will we know if it is him?"

"I've seen him, remember, in person. It was a quick look, but I'll be able to spot him again in a crowd."

"Okay. Here's your chance."

Another car pulled to a halt next to Emad's. Three men stepped out of the back seat and stood talking to the terrorist leader through the open window of his vehicle. Ara's speaker couldn't pick up what they were saying. Bolan brought out his field glasses and peered across the distance, examining the features of each of the men.

"That's him, the one nearest the window," Bolan said. "Let's go."

"We're moving in!" Abi said into the radio microphone.

At that moment Nabil Aman and one of the other men got in the back seat of Emad's car. The man who remained standing glanced up when he heard the shriek of tires and was the first to spot the two vehicles homing in on them from either side. He grabbed into his shirtfront and withdrew a large handgun, which he leveled at the closer car, carrying Abi's men, and started firing. The shots were large caliber, punching holes in the windshield, and the agency man yanked the car sideways, where it halted suddenly. Bolan reached out the window with the Desert Eagle as Abi slammed on the brakes. He fired at the gunman once, but it was just as the car lurched to the left, and the .44-caliber blast sailed inches from the gunman's body.

The terrorist redirected his aim at the second car, and Bolan fired again, twice, as Abi brought their vehicle to a stop. The gunman curled over his belly and fell to the pavement.

There was a blast of machine-gun fire from inside Emad's car. It blew out the back window and peppered both cars and the parking lot with rounds, forcing Bolan and Abi to duck behind the dashboard. Then the soldier heard the screaming of rubber as Emad's car roared forward, bounced up the curb and onto the walkway, which had emptied of people. It crashed into the front doors with an explosion of shattered glass, rending the aluminum frame and roaring into the lobby of the hotel, where it disappeared from view. They heard it crash.

"Stay here and monitor Ara," Bolan said as he jumped from Abi's vehicle, snatching up the Heckler & Koch MP-5 A-3 and stalking in the direction of the second car. The door on the far side of the vehicle opened, and he saw a figure crawling out. Then a face appeared over the ear of the vehicle, aiming an AK-47 at Abi's men. He hadn't spotted the Executioner approaching on foot. He triggered a blast in the direction of the car, puncturing metal body panels, and Bolan targeted him with the MP-5 A-3. The Egyptian spotted movement out of the corner of his eye and turned. By that time the subgun had commenced to speak. The man flung his arms out, tossing away the Soviet assault rifle as his chest was stitched with bloody holes.

Bolan sprinted to the car, confirming it was now empty, and headed into the lobby, through the cavernous opening created by Emad's car. He spotted it, squashed against the far wall. There was a path of ruin behind it—chairs, ashtrays and plants were smashed and scattered on the carpeting. Hotel guests and staff cowered in every corner of the expansive, plush lobby.

There was no movement in the car and the doors stood

open. Bolan approached quickly but cautiously. No one was inside.

"They took the elevator just a few seconds ago." A man in a suit, British by his accent, lay on his back on the floor nearby. He was bleeding from a hole in his stomach. "I got in their way."

Bolan spotted the elevator and raced for it, watching the lighted display. The elevator was still ascending, and it stopped at the nineteenth floor.

He couldn't take a chance using the elevator. They might be waiting when the doors opened, perhaps blast out the cables when he was en route. He jogged to the stairs and started up, full of misgivings—he couldn't even be sure they would stay on the nineteenth floor.

He pulled the walkie-talkie from his belt. "Abi, I'm following them up. What are they saying?"

"Emad found the transmitter just a second ago. Ara's getting a damn hard time. You'd better hurry!"

It took him under two minutes to reach the nineteenth floor, and he slowed as he approached the landing. There was a narrow window in the door to the hallway, and he peered out. He couldn't see a thing.

He stepped into the hallway on full alert, ears tuned but hearing nothing.

Until he heard the breathing.

It came from around a corner ahead. Someone was there, trying to be silent, coming closer with silent steps but gasping hard from exertion. In the quiet hallway the stalker could be heard a long way off. The Executioner waited for him to show himself.

Then he heard a door opening and a woman's scream.

He launched himself around the corner into the hallway. A woman had just emerged from her room and spotted the Egyptian gunman, brandishing his assault rifle, which was now turned on her.

So when the stalker saw Bolan he wasn't properly positioned to defend himself. The subgun in the Executioner's hand rattled and a half-dozen rounds mangled the gunman's chest, punching him to the floor. The woman's screams rose to hysterical wails, and she retreated into her room, slamming the door.

"Belasko!" The voice was Ara's, and it was followed by the sound of flesh meeting flesh, the kind of impact that broke a person's jaw. The soldier followed it, pointing the way with the MP-5 A-3. Then there was the sound of a gunshot. Bolan broke into a run, rounded the next corner, found the hallway clear and ran on. Ahead a set of double doors stood open.

Slowing his approach, Bolan traded the MP-5 A-3 for the Desert Eagle, slinging the subgun. A hand with a pistol of similar caliber appeared out the door, and a face came into view a moment later. At that moment the Executioner fired, and the harsh retort of the .44 Magnum gun was followed by a screech of pain from the victim. He tumbled into the hall, a large section of flesh torn from his face by the Magnum round. There was enough of the face left, however, for Bolan to determine it wasn't Emad, just one of his underlings. He fired a second time, and the screeching stopped.

"Show yourself, Belasko, or I put a slug in my traitorous little sister."

The voice was Emad's, and it came from within the room. Bolan stepped into the open and aimed the Desert Eagle at the terrorist. The man stood across what was a small banquet or meeting room, currently empty except for stacks of chairs set against a far wall.

Nabil Aman was on the floor, his knee bloody and shredded as if it had been chewed by a wild animal. His eyes were glazed with pain.

Ara Emad was kneeling on the floor, looking at Bolan, and a few steps behind her was her brother, with an AK-47 leveled at the back of her skull, his finger on the trigger.

He had removed his outer shirt, and bars of plastique and sticks of dynamite were massed together around his back and stomach with yards of black tape. His other hand grasped a small plastic device no larger than a book of matches, linked to his body with a thin wire.

"Hear that, Belasko?" Emad's eyes went to the ceiling. Then Bolan heard the thumping of loud music coming from above. "There's a cocktail reception going on. American investors, being wooed into Egypt by sleazy big business. They're all going, Belasko. And we're going with them."

"He's going to kill us all!" Aman roared.

"My friend Nabil wasn't as dedicated as he pretended to be. But I am. I've always been prepared to die for the cause." He stared at Bolan. "Are you?"

"No," the Executioner replied, and his finger closed on the trigger of the Desert Eagle, which blasted monstrously in the close walls.

Emad's hand was squeezing on the plastic controller, and he raised it to his face, staring at the dangling wire, chopped in two by the blast from the .44 Magnum round. Then he whipped the AK-47 in Bolan's direction, already firing, and Ara fell face-forward on the floor. Bolan triggered the Desert Eagle repeatedly, watching Emad's face disintegrate into blood and ruin. The body flopped into a sitting position and fell back against the wall.

"All right, hero, put it down. Put them all down."

Nabil Aman had a Glock 17 handgun directed at Bolan, and he was inching toward the door.

Bolan made no move to comply.

"I said put them down. If you don't, I shoot the girl."

The soldier glanced at Ara's prostrate form. A shaft of blood across her skull showed the path of the Kalashnikov round that downed her. But she was breathing. She was alive.

"All right," Bolan said. He dropped the Desert Eagle

and it bounced on the carpeted floor with a heavy thump. Then he launched himself at Aman.

The terrormonger fired the Glock, and Bolan felt the wind of the round's passage inches from his body. Before the second bullet could be triggered, his foot hit Aman's gun hand and the weapon went flying through the air, hitting the wall and falling to the floor. The soldier slammed the side of his foot into his adversary's skull, leveraging his weight behind the blow, and Aman's skull popped. He grabbed the Beretta 93-R from its armpit holster and sent a burst of 9 mm parabellum rounds through Aman's chest.

The Holy Voice was exterminated.

**Don't miss out on the action in these titles featuring
THE EXECUTIONER®, STONY MAN™ and SUPERBOLAN®!**

The Red Dragon Trilogy

#64210	FIRE LASH	$3.75 U.S. ☐
		$4.25 CAN. ☐
#64211	STEEL CLAWS	$3.75 U.S. ☐
		$4.25 CAN. ☐
#64212	RIDE THE BEAST	$3.75 U.S. ☐
		$4.25 CAN. ☐

Stony Man™

#61907	THE PERISHING GAME	$5.50 U.S. ☐
		$6.50 CAN. ☐
#61908	BIRD OF PREY	$5.50 U.S. ☐
		$6.50 CAN. ☐
#61909	SKYLANCE	$5.50 U.S. ☐
		$6.50 CAN. ☐

SuperBolan®

#61448	DEAD CENTER	$5.50 U.S. ☐
		$6.50 CAN. ☐
#61449	TOOTH AND CLAW	$5.50 U.S. ☐
		$6.50 CAN. ☐
#61450	RED HEAT	$5.50 U.S. ☐
		$6.50 CAN. ☐

(limited quantities available on certain titles)

TOTAL AMOUNT	$
POSTAGE & HANDLING	$
($1.00 for one book, 50¢ for each additional)	
APPLICABLE TAXES*	$_____
TOTAL PAYABLE	$_____
(check or money order—please do not send cash)	

To order, complete this form and send it, along with a check or money order for the total above, payable to Gold Eagle Books, to: **In the U.S.:** 3010 Walden Avenue, P.O. Box 9077, Buffalo, NY 14269-9077; **In Canada:** P.O. Box 636, Fort Erie, Ontario, L2A 5X3.

Name:_____

Address:_____ City:_____

State/Prov.:_____ Zip/Postal Code: _____

*New York residents remit applicable sales taxes.
Canadian residents remit applicable GST and provincial taxes.

GEBACK17

When all is lost, there is always the future

JAMES AXLER

DEATH LANDS®

Skydark

It's now generations after the firestorm that nearly consumed the earth, and fear spreads like wildfire when an army of mutants goes on the rampage. Ryan Cawdor must unite the baronies to defeat a charismatic and powerful mutant lord, or all will perish.

In the Deathlands, the future is just beginning.

The Destroyer takes on a plague of invisible insects—as the exterminator

#107 Feast or Famine

Created by
WARREN MURPHY
and RICHARD SAPIR

Is the insect kingdom mobilizing to reclaim the planet...or is something entirely different behind it all? Unless the Destroyer can combat this disaster, a whole nation may start dropping like flies.

Look for it in April wherever Gold Eagle books are sold.

Don't miss out on the action in these titles!

Deathlands

#62530	CROSSWAYS	$4.99 U.S.	☐
		$5.50 CAN.	☐
#62532	CIRCLE THRICE	$5.50 U.S.	☐
		$6.50 CAN.	☐
#62533	ECLIPSE AT NOON	$5.50 U.S.	☐
		$6.50 CAN.	☐
#62534	STONEFACE	$5.50 U.S.	☐
		$6.50 CAN.	☐

The Destroyer

#63210	HIGH PRIESTESS	$4.99	☐
#63218	ENGINES OF DESTRUCTION	$5.50 U.S.	☐
		$6.50 CAN.	☐
#63219	ANGRY WHITE MAILMEN	$5.50 U.S.	☐
		$6.50 CAN.	☐
#63220	SCORCHED EARTH	$5.50 U.S.	☐
		$6.50 CAN.	☐

(limited quantities available on certain titles)

TOTAL AMOUNT	$
POSTAGE & HANDLING	$
($1.00 for one book, 50¢ for each additional)	
APPLICABLE TAXES*	$_____
TOTAL PAYABLE	$_____
(check or money order—please do not send cash)	

To order, complete this form and send it, along with a check or money order for the total above, payable to Gold Eagle Books, to: **In the U.S.:** 3010 Walden Avenue, P.O. Box 9077, Buffalo, NY 14269-9077; **In Canada:** P.O. Box 636, Fort Erie, Ontario, L2A 5X3.

Name:_____

Address:_____ City:_____

State/Prov.:_____ Zip/Postal Code:_____

*New York residents remit applicable sales taxes.
 Canadian residents remit applicable GST and provincial taxes.

GEBACK17A